THE SECRET OF SEVEN MILE ISLAND

DAN THOMPSON

THE SECRET OF

SEVEN MILE ISLAND

CONTENTS

PROLOGUE

This story details how a family's vacation in 1985 became entwined with events that occurred forty years earlier.

Elizabeth and Mark Sanders, along with their children, Lisa, Johnny, and Wayne, planned to spend a fun and relaxing summer at the New Jersey shore. Specifically, they were headed to the large bayfront home of Elizabeth's parents, Christine and Dylan Masters, on a beautiful barrier island called *Seven Mile Island.*

This trip began with the family thoroughly enjoying life at the beach, but the holiday soon turned into a historical adventure full of mystery, deceit, murder, action, discovery, and camaraderie.

Although some authentic dates, events, names, and places are referenced from time to time, this intriguing and imaginative tale adds just enough twists and turns to frustrate historians and their long-established portrayals of the Second World War and the fall of Germany's Third Reich.

Let the adventure begin…

With the rain and the thunder
A flash of lightning
Buried down upon the cove

The sands cried out
As the waves crashed in
Trying desperately to hold

Cursed by Poseidon
Engulfed by the sea
There was no safe port to tie

With swells so large
And winds so fierce
No vessels could survive

When the storm died out
All had changed
The island was crushed and bruised

But buried beneath
Was a frightful tale
Only one could claim as true

Iceland
Bergen, Norway
Bremen, Germany
Great Britain
Europe
North America
Berlin, Germany
Atlantic Ocean
United States
Seven Mile Island
Asia
Gulf Stream
Equatorial Current
Africa
South America
Cape Verde Islands
Patagonia, Argentina

CHAPTER 1
UNNAMED STORM

{Seven Mile Island, NJ – June 1945}

When the sun began to rise over the ocean, the calm surf waters off the shoreline of Seven Mile Island reflected brilliant rays of colorful hopes and dreams. With summer solstice quickly approaching, June 20, 1945, was destined to be a gorgeous day with warm and sunny weather. There was no indication that this small barrier island off the southeastern coast of New Jersey would soon face a challenge of monumental proportions.

As the day progressed, the skies over the Atlantic turned fiercely dark, and then God's fury struck in the shape of a massive coastal storm. Savage waves crashed into the beaches with the sound of thunder, redistributing the sand as mighty winds ripped the island's small structures from their foundations. The island's small population was helpless for the next forty-eight hours as the unnatural forces changed the normally peaceful swells into frenzies of merciless breakers.

Huge tsunamic surges reshaped and transformed the northern fringes of the island, leaving mountains of sand in areas where tidal pools previously existed and seawater where bungalows, cottages, and houses once stood. Even the northern inlet that connected the bay with the ocean was reshaped from a once-narrow channel into an expansive aquatic basin.

When the unnamed storm subsided, the residents of Avalon — a small town located on the island's north side — could not believe the extent of the damage. Nothing was left untouched. The beaches, the dunes, the bridges, the seawalls, and all other structures were ravaged. For the second time in the past nine months, the island had fallen victim to a destructive weather event. Although it could have been a knockout blow to the town's four hundred year-round residents, the locals persevered and pledged to rebuild.

In the immediate aftermath of this latest storm, a fascinating phenomenon occurred. Thousands of turtles arrived on the island. The town's residents could not remember a time when so many of the beautiful creatures traversed the sandy landscape. The impact was immediate and lasting.

Locals began associating the town's motto, "Cooler by the Mile," with the amazing influx of turtles. Although this old catchphrase was commonly associated with the cool breezes that gently caressed Seven Mile Island during the hot summer months, the residents reckoned that the calm nature of the small creatures carried an unspoken message of hope: "Stay cool. Stay strong. All is not lost."

This helped the locals maintain their composure as they rebuilt their community and to be courageous as they endured the uncertainties and anguish of the nation's ongoing involvement in the Second World War.

CHAPTER 2
FÜHRER'S BIRTHDAY PLAN

{Germany – April 1945}

On the morning of April 20, 1945, Adolf Hitler was presented a large cake by several of his closest advisors and officers in celebration of the German leader's fifty-sixth birthday. The occasion was not festive, as the gathering occurred deep in a dreary subterranean bunker complex near the Reich Chancellery in Berlin, Germany.

By this stage of World War II, most of Hitler's officers thought that Germany could no longer win the war. While Hitler understood that his previous military gains throughout Europe between 1938 and 1943 were being lost to the Soviet and Allied forces, he still believed there was hope for victory. For Hitler, the concept of surrender was impossible. To those present that day, Hitler pledged, "I will never stop fighting!"

Addressing the group, Hitler outlined a surprising and unthinkable scheme that would immediately move the Nazi leader's headquarters from Berlin to a faraway sanctuary hidden in South America. He told the group that over the past decade, he had secretly implemented a plan to colonize the country of Argentina. He commented, "There are Argentinian political and military leaders who have pledged their allegiance to the German cause and fully support my preparations for a new world order."

Hitler declared that Argentina's celebrated general and Nazi sympathizer Juan Domingo Perón had been a most helpful confidant and ally after Hitler became the uncontested leader of Germany in 1934. He continued, "The Kriegsmarine [German Navy] has performed flawlessly in transporting vast military, industrial, and civilian supplies to Argentina. We have also relocated thousands of Germans to the region who are thriving in newly constructed German communities. And I'm pleased to report that these loyal pioneers have begun large-scale manufacturing operations in support of our cause!"

Hitler then described the merits of the move in great detail before emphasizing, "Everyone gathered here will serve in my new fortified headquarters. It sits on the banks of a glorious mountain lake located in Patagonia, Argentina. Together, we will continue to expand the German empire throughout the Americas."

He slowly and deliberately made eye contact with every person in the room before continuing. "My friends, have no fear. I will lead you and all Germans throughout the world to ultimate success!"

In response, the small group displayed their obedience to the German dictator by saluting him while saying, "Heil Hitler!"

At that moment, a young Luftwaffe [German air force] pilot knocked on the door of the conference room, saluted his leader, and then cautiously approached. "Mein Führer [My

Leader], everything is set for the transport and voyage as you instructed. The special cargo has been loaded onto the four XXI-A class U-boats. The submarine crews await your arrival at the Valentin submarine base." The pilot then looked directly at Hitler and said sincerely, "Mein Führer, I would also like to wish you a very happy birthday."

Hitler acknowledged the kind words with a slight nod of his head. He then turned to his confidants, raised his glass into the air, and proclaimed, "To the Fatherland and ultimate victory!" After emptying his small glass, he ordered, "All is done here. Everyone to the planes!"

As his party began to exit the conference room and ascend the stairs to leave the subterranean bunker, Hitler addressed a man and woman who stood at the rear of the room. Interestingly, they looked strikingly like Hitler and his longtime companion, Eva Braun.

"You have your orders. By fulfilling this mission, you will have performed the ultimate service for preserving the German Reich. Your sacrifice will be forever honored, and the Fatherland will thrive!" Hitler then left the room and exited the bunker for the last time.

The exclusive party was ushered to a makeshift runway at Berlin's Brandenburg Gate, where three airplanes awaited. This eighteenth-century monument was normally used by the Nazi Party to host large political and military gatherings. But on this day, it was being used as a top-secret airstrip.

After Hitler and his officers boarded one of his personal transport planes, a seventeen-passenger, three-engine Junkers Ju-52 aircraft registered as the D-2600, the aircraft swiftly propelled down the long plaza square escorted by two Luftwaffe fighters for protection. The three aircraft then ascended into the skies above Berlin and soared toward the U-boat bunker base on the Weser River in northwestern Germany.

After safely arriving at the base, Hitler awarded the Luftwaffe pilots with Nazi Germany's highest military award.

"It is my honor to present each of you with the Iron Cross for your heroic skills and bravery today." The Iron Cross was normally reserved for the highest-ranking German officers. But on this day, Hitler understood that the pilots had unknowingly guided the elite group out of Berlin just hours before the Soviet and Allied troops entered the German capital.

Just before Hitler dismissed the honored airmen, he earnestly commanded, "Be passionate and continue to fight for the German nation!"

Hitler's officers and guests boarded the four Wunderwaffe [wonder weapon] U-boats, and the convoy departed toward the North Sea. Surprisingly, while these unique vessels were constructed specifically for the German leader, this was the first time that the XXI-A class U-boats were seeing any kind of naval action.

These special diesel-electric super-submarines were designed to be the most advanced submersible vessels ever launched. With their superior batteries, silent and powerful engines, and stealthy construction, these U-boats could move faster than any other undersea vessels in the world. They could also travel fully submerged for thousands of miles at a time, making these super-submarines almost undetectable to Germany's enemies.

As well as sophisticated armaments of torpedoes, anti-aircraft guns, and powerful machine guns, the four U-boats also carried a top-secret cargo of gold bars!

Several months earlier, Hitler ordered Germany's national bank — the Reichsbank — to transport vast quantities of gold bars to the U-boat bunker. Subsequently, the valuable freight was loaded onto the four U-boats, where it remained protected by a select group of armed personnel.

The origin of the gold was not documented, but it was likely that Hitler's evil regime unethically and forcibly obtained it. For more than ten years, his followers committed horrendous crimes against humanity, including the theft of unimaginable levels of property from individuals, businesses, and the governments of countries that were invaded by the German military machine.

As the U-boats maneuvered into the North Sea, the captain of the last vessel in the convoy, Wilhelm Yeager, expressed his private thoughts about this voyage to his young lieutenant commander, 24-year-old Franz Schmidt. "May God be with us on this crazy voyage, Franz. All reports indicate that the war is lost and Germany is defeated."

Franz responded with surprise and anger. "With all due respect, sir, our Führer is directing this convoy, and he told us that this special mission will lead to ultimate victory. As your friend, I urge you to command this vessel as a dedicated and committed servant of the Reich."

The captain quietly steered the submarine away from the German homeland. Yeager was frustrated that his naïve subordinate was unable to comprehend that Germany was on the verge of defeat. Additionally, the captain knew that his assigned submarine had failed its final performance inspection two days earlier, a fact that was not shared with the younger officer.

The 251-foot-long submarine was nearly impossible to control and maneuver in open waters. This difficulty was primarily due to the reduction in crew from fifty-seven down to thirty — a necessity to accommodate the vast and weighty cargo of gold bars. While the naval inspectors had certified that the U-boat was ready for active service, Captain Yeager knew that Hitler's secret police called the Gestapo, simply forced the inspectors to alter their findings to show that his vessel had safely passed the inspection.

With that in mind, the aggravated and disheartened captain quietly muttered, "Sure, we will be fine, Franz, especially since our fearless Führer has blessed this voyage. Hah!"

CHAPTER 3
SUMMER VACATION BEGINS

{New Jersey – June 1985}

"Honey, how did you do on your history test?" Elizabeth asked her twelve-year-old son Wayne after he and his twin brother, Johnny, walked through the front door of their Moorestown, New Jersey home.

"Well, let's put it this way," he answered tentatively with a grin, "I think I did great considering that I learned a marking period's worth of World War Two history in one night, but only fair compared to Johnny! But one thing's for sure, it's on to the seventh grade for me ... Whoo-hoo!!!!"

Elizabeth smiled as she patted Wayne's broad shoulders and turned toward Johnny, asking anxiously, "And how did *you* do?"

In meticulous fashion, Johnny explained how he not only answered all of the exam questions correctly but also received bonus points for being the only student to identify the author and title of his two history textbooks.

With that, Wayne interjected, "Stop bragging, Johnny! We all know that you're the *bookworm*. But let's see how all of that studying helps you with beach volleyball this summer."

At that moment, sensing that her boys were about to engage in one of their notorious tickling/wrestling battles, Elizabeth quickly said, "Well, boys, I'm proud of both of you. I know that you'll do great next year at the Moorestown Middle School." Then she looked directly at Wayne and added with a slight smile, "And I'll definitely be expecting more studying from you!"

Johnny burst out laughing when he heard his mom's exaggerated "threat" to his brother, knowing that she was really joking. In fact, Wayne was a very good student who had achieved all As and Bs on his final sixth-grade report card. On the other hand, Johnny was an excellent student who earned straight As for the entire school year.

Turning to Wayne, Johnny said, "Great job this year. We made it. Now, let's have a blast this summer."

As the boys were about to run out of their house to the large backyard, Wayne turned toward his mom and asked, "Mom, what time are we leaving for Grandma and Grandpa's house at the shore tomorrow?"

Elizabeth responded, "Very early in the morning." Adding, "Don't play too long, boys. You still need to finish packing your bags because your father wants the car loaded tonight. . . . And don't forget your swimsuits!"

———

Early the next morning, Mark Sanders could be heard shouting, "Come on, let's go! Liz, did you find the kid's water skis?"

"They're already packed," Liz responded as she handed Mark the last of the shore-bound gear.

"Where's Lisa?" Mark asked, referring to their fifteen-year-old daughter.

"She's saying goodbye to Sean," explained Elizabeth.

"My baby girl sure has grown up fast," said Mark with a sigh.

"She's *our* girl, Mark."

He leaned over and kissed his wife of sixteen years on the forehead as if asking for forgiveness for the slip.

After they walked back into their two-story house, Mark ensured that all the windows and doors were locked and that the air conditioner's thermostat was set at 74 degrees. "That should be cool enough to keep our spoiled cat very comfortable." Then he asked, "Honey, who did you say is going to feed Muffy this summer?"

At that moment, Lisa hung up the telephone and chimed in. "Don't worry, Dad. Sean is going to stop over every night at five o'clock to feed the cat."

Mark turned to Liz. "Seriously? Her boyfriend's taking care of our cat this summer?"

Liz simply smiled and said, "Hang in there, Mark. Everything will be fine." Liz understood that her husband was not used to their daughter being a teenager.

At exactly nine that Saturday morning, the Sanders' Jeep Grand Wagoneer left their modest home in Moorestown and headed down Route 73 toward the Jersey Shore. The traffic was bumper-to-bumper on the industrial highway, but it was a beautiful sunny day with temperatures in the low eighties. And because there was not a trace of humidity in the air, Mark felt cool, relaxed, and happy. That is until he heard his daughter ask, "Dad, can we listen to some music instead of this weird radio station?"

Wayne then added, "Yeah, Dad. Something cool, please."

Mark responded, "Hey, I really like this station. If you kids would actually listen to AM News Radio instead of that noise you call music, you'd be amazed how much you could learn."

Even so, after the local traffic report was announced, Mark consented to his children's wishes and turned the car stereo control knob to a classic rock station. In fact, he really wasn't bothered by the change since he and Liz both loved classic rock music, especially the Beatles, the Beach Boys, and the Rolling Stones. And Mark also liked the idea of kicking the summer off with some upbeat tunes.

Once the kids were satisfied with the great music resonating from the speakers, Mark decided to exit the congested highway in favor of several rural and picturesque roads that passed through the towns of Folsom, Buena Vista, Woodbine, and Clermont. By doing so, he avoided most of the stressful traffic, and the family was able to enjoy the beautiful South Jersey landscape that included large farms, woodlands, railroads, marshlands, and waterways.

As the Jeep proceeded down Route 9, a winding coastal highway that headed directly to the exit for Seven Mile Island, Elizabeth turned toward her children and launched into a long speech. The topic concerned the "dos and don'ts" at Grandma and Grandpa's shore house.

"OK, boys, remember that your grandparents are both over 65 years old. And even though they act young, you cannot ask them to go waterskiing again this year. Grandpa is still complaining that his back hurts from last summer's escapades!"

With that, Wayne and Johnny both burst out laughing, remembering how they had convinced their grandfather to ride the inner tube behind their father's twenty-foot Boston Whaler motorboat the previous summer.

"But Mom," Wayne rationalized with a smirk, "Grandpa insisted on trying and —"

Elizabeth interrupted him. "Wayne, I don't want to hear it. You, Johnny, and Lisa are expected to help your grandparents around the house. And there is to be absolutely no kissing up to them in hopes of getting money. Do you understand?"

As both boys nodded affirmatively, Mark added that he would be keeping an eye on them to make certain that they were holding to it.

Lisa frustratingly agonized to her mom, "But I already have a job lined up to serve breakfast at the Fishin' Pier Grille. Do I still have to work around the house?"

Elizabeth responded with a caring nod. "We'll see. It depends on how often you waitress. But I'm certain it won't be a hardship for you to help wash and dry the dishes after meals occasionally."

Mark sat silently in the driver's seat as Elizabeth continued to lecture the children. Deep down, he knew that the kids would help out since they truly loved their grandparents. Even so, he also understood that the kids would be very busy with their extensive summer plans. The boys had already informed everyone that they would be swimming, surfing, waterskiing, playing volleyball at the beach, playing water polo in the bay, and fishing too! The boys also wanted to try crabbing in the bay, using their grandfather's dinghy. Wayne had expressed earlier in the week that he and his brother hoped to catch and sell crabs throughout the summer as a way of earning some extra spending money.

As Mark continued to drive toward Seven Mile Island, he sensed that the children weren't entirely listening to Liz. He guessed that they were likely daydreaming about an awesome summer full of fun adventures. Even so, he hoped that they heard the highlights since his wife's pre-vacation lecture was simply her way of reminding the kids to be on their best behavior.

At the intersection of Route 9 and Avalon Boulevard, Mark stopped his Jeep at the red traffic light. He turned to his wife and gently said, "Hang in there, Liz. Everything will be just fine." When the traffic light changed to green, Mark turned left onto the four-and-a-half-mile scenic causeway, Avalon Boulevard. While driving over the tallest of four causeway bridges, the family truly enjoyed amazing views of the salt marshlands, bay waters, and numerous boats along this last stretch to Seven Mile Island.

CHAPTER 4
CONVOY ON THE MOVE

{Atlantic Ocean — April/June 1945}

Hitler's U-boat convoy slowly navigated in stealth mode through the dangerous North Sea. The captains of the four vessels used great skill to escape detection by the Allied naval vessels and to avoid colliding with any of the hundreds of floating mines that were set by the Royal Navy.

After almost two days of purposely slow undersea travel, the convoy quietly entered another secret German naval base located in Bergen, Norway. Though the Allies had conducted several bombing raids near the base over the past two years, the concealed and protected submarine pens were not damaged. Because of this, Hitler's four U-boats remained safe while additional fuel and provisions were secured for the long voyage to Argentina.

During the journey, one of the U-boat captains notified the others that his vessel's snorkeling device was not working properly and required repairs. This important pole-like apparatus enabled a U-boat to operate while submerged. The primary task of the snorkel was to reach high above a submerged sub's upper deck and control platform. Once extended above the sea surface, it would channel fresh air back down into the vessel. This function was extremely important not only for the comfort of the U-boat passengers but also for recharging the many batteries required to operate the XXI-A class U-boats.

On April 30, 1945, the crucial repair work was completed. While Hitler, his officers, and the crew discussed plans for continuing the journey, one of the U-boat radio crewmen politely notified the group of a breaking news broadcast that declared that Adolf Hitler had died in his bunker in Berlin, Germany.

"My plan is a success!" Hitler boasted to his officers. "The Soviets and Allies now believe that the two actors who committed suicide in my bunker are actually Eva and me. They are all fools."

Then he explained, "Do not be alarmed. I've left orders for Joseph Goebbels to temporarily assume the role of Chancellor and for Admiral Karl Dönitz to serve as the interim Supreme Commander of the Armed Forces. They will direct our government and war effort until we reach Argentina. Once we arrive in the new Fatherland, I will resume directing our mighty forces."

Early the next morning, with the world believing that Adolf Hitler was dead, the elusive leader ordered the convoy to quickly depart from Norway.

After a smooth and uneventful ride toward Iceland, the U-boats turned south and began the 7,500-mile quest through the Atlantic Ocean toward Argentina. The small convoy was scheduled to make only one stop along the way, a rendezvous at the Cape Verde Islands.

During the first few days of the journey, the officers and passengers were jubilant, trusting they were destined for triumph and great rewards in the new Fatherland. But they were gravely incorrect. By May 8, everyone on board knew that the so-called super submarines were not entirely seaworthy. All four captains openly complained that the vessels handled like "drifting coffins" because of their excessive weight and insufficient power.

To add to their problems, communications between the vessels were problematic because the radio transmitting equipment was malfunctioning. For this reason, the four submarines filled their ballast tanks with air and briefly surfaced.

While motoring on the Atlantic's surface, the four U-boats raised their communication aerials. The Führer and his party listened to a long-range radio broadcast announcer declare, "Germany has surrendered! Germany has surrendered to the Allied forces. The European war is over!"

Hitler did not speak for several minutes. He was visibly shaken. The broadcaster said that Joseph Goebbels had committed suicide on May 1 and that on May 7, Admiral Karl Dönitz had authorized Germany's surrender to the Allied forces.

Incredibly, Hitler quickly recovered from his initial shock. In an attempt to display continued strength to the troubled officers and U-boat passengers, he commanded, "Do not worry. This means nothing. The Third Reich is alive and well. We will be in Argentina soon!"

For the next four weeks, the resubmerged U-boat convoy headed southward toward the strategic Cape Verde Islands. This group of ten volcanic islands was located in the Atlantic Ocean, 350 miles west of the African continent. The convoy occupants were eager to reach this destination, but because of their heavy cargo, the U-boats operated poorly, and progress was slow.

Many passengers were visibly dejected by the news of Germany's surrender. To make matters worse, the snorkel devices were not providing enough fresh air into the vessels, and numerous occupants became ill.

When the convoy finally reached its destination, the four U-boats surfaced and anchored in a deep-water cove near one of the remote mountainous islands. Hitler ordered several seamen to disembark and secure supplies from a trusted islander. During this brief stoppage, the officers, crew, and passengers enjoyed the island's clean air, warmer temperatures, and fresh fruits and vegetables. Hitler urged everyone to eat, drink, and enjoy the temporary rest. "But understand, we will not be staying long."

Although most of Hitler's officers appreciated the restful stopover, some quietly expressed grave concerns that the short stay was an unnecessary risk. They feared that if any outsiders saw the four large German U-boats, they would assume that this flotilla had offensive intentions and were a threat.

Standing on the deck of his U-boat, Captain Yeager spoke in a low voice to one of his trusted officers. "It's almost certain that if we are discovered, the Allies will launch a quick and fatal strike without first asking questions." Yeager shook his head in frustration and added, "The entire world believes that Germany has surrendered. We should not be here!"

CHAPTER 5
WELCOME TO THE ISLAND

"What a gorgeous Saturday morning!" said Dylan Masters as he walked into his house and greeted Christine, his wife of forty years. "I just can't get over how low the tide waters are today. Probably the lowest I've seen in ten years."

Christine responded from the kitchen of their large five-bedroom home on a unique three-acre bayfront peninsula near the northwestern tip of the island. "Oh, it's probably related to the recent storm and the full moon. What were you doing at the dock, dear?"

"Oh, I was just lubricating the boat line pulleys," said Dylan as he pointed outside toward the lines that held his boat securely to the dock. "They were really corroded. Considering the extreme tide changes, I don't want to risk the lines getting stuck. If that happens, the increased tension could damage our boat and dock! By the way, what time did you say that Elizabeth and the troops are arriving?"

Christine walked over to her husband, who was gazing out the large family room window toward the waterfront. "Liz told me that they were leaving Moorestown at nine and hoped to arrive around eleven. It all depends on how much traffic they hit."

Dylan adjusted his wristwatch and noticed that it was already half past eleven. "Well, they should be here any minute now." Then he smiled at his wife and said, "Just think of it: three active kids in this old castle for the entire summer! Not to mention Liz and Mark. I hope that Liz can actually relax a bit while she's here instead of constantly worrying about her children … and us more mature folks." Dylan, known as Grandpa to the Sanders' children, shook his head and laughed in amusement. "Ugh, mature folks."

Christine gave her husband a heartfelt hug and said, "Come on, you old fool. We have more to do before they arrive." With that, she kissed Dylan on the cheek, and they exited the family room's sliding glass door onto an expansive exterior wood deck. Once outside, Christine and Dylan filled their time by placing several chairs around a large picnic table, knowing that they would soon need to serve lunch to their summer guests.

A short time later, Grandpa merrily greeted the newcomers. "Well, hello there. Welcome to the Island!" As the Sanders family exited their vehicle after the two-and-a-half-hour journey, he added, "How was the drive, Mark?"

Mark responded, "A little longer than normal, but overall, it was just fine."

Elizabeth chimed in by expressing that it was a very relaxing drive on such a beautiful summer day.

While Elizabeth and her parents warmly greeted one another, Wayne and Johnny ran up to their grandpa to say hello. "OK, you two," Grandpa said in mock seriousness.

"Let's get one thing straight before we commence with the summer festivities. Let it be known that this year, I will get up on those darn water skis! But there is no way that you will ever get me in that inner tube contraption again!"

With that, the entire family broke into a great roar of laughter that momentarily drowned out the ever-present sound of the abundant bird population that thrived throughout the Island and nearby wetlands.

"All right, kids," said Grandma. "As soon as your bags are unloaded and placed up in your rooms, I want everyone to gather on the back deck for an Avalon-style grand lunch. And don't worry, Lisa, I have plenty of fruit, salad, and diet sodas so that you can maintain your cute figure!"

With that, Lisa blushed and embarrassingly responded, "Grandma!" Elizabeth looked at her attractive five-foot-five daughter and winked as if to tell her that Grandma only meant well.

Lisa added with a big grin. "Thanks, Grandma. I'll definitely be watching my calories this summer. But it may be a challenge since I'll be working at the Fishin' Pier Grille, and you know how much I love the food there!"

A short time later, the family congregated on the back deck for some tasty food and beverages. The Masters' neighbors, Bob and Lilly Bloomfield, joined them for lunch. The group had a nice time catching up, describing the highlights in their lives since the previous summer. They also discussed a recent hurricane that had caused extensive damage across the island, including to the nearby bridge at Townsends Inlet. This important span connected Seven Mile Island with Sea Isle City, located on Ludlam Island.

Turning toward Mark, Bob asked, "Have you had a chance to tour the island since you arrived? The recent storm really caused some havoc around here."

"Not yet. But my local newspaper printed an article in the latest issue indicating that the damages were severe."

Bob pointed to the inlet bridge that was about a quarter mile to the northeast of Dylan's deck. "If you really focus, you can see some of the structural damage from here!"

After gazing toward the bridge for a few seconds, Mark responded, "Wow. It certainly looks like the bridge was hit hard."

Bob and Mark had met several years earlier and instantly felt a strong bond. Bob was close to twenty years older than Mark, and each greatly admired the other, most likely because they had served in the US Navy after graduating college. These two strong men were brothers-in-arms and like long-lost comrades. They also loved spending time on their boats, which enhanced their friendship.

As the group continued to chat, Bob asked Mark and Dylan if they wanted to go out on his boat for a tour around the island after lunch. Dylan said, "That sounds like a marvelous idea. It'll give us a chance to see how Mother Nature is really in charge!"

Sensing one of her husband's notorious speeches concerning his displeasure with the overdevelopment of some of South Jersey's barrier islands, Elizabeth spoke up. "Dylan, you better eat your lobster roll before that greenhead fly decides it's his!"

Waving the large flying insect away from his plate, Dylan bit into his delicious sandwich and followed it down with a satisfying swig of ice-cold lemonade. "Ah, that's good," he said with an expression of pure delight.

At 2:30 p.m., the men walked a few hundred yards south to Bob's bayside home, where they boarded his twenty-eight-foot Grady-White fishing boat. Johnny and Wayne tagged behind after Bob had enthusiastically invited the boys to come along.

Before his sons boarded the boat, Mark handed each boy a life jacket and warned, "Behave yourselves, *comprende?*" Both boys simply smiled and gave their dad a thumbs-up.

The Grady-White traveled a short distance to the north and then turned eastward into Townsends Inlet. "So, Dylan, in all your years here on Seven Mile Island, have you witnessed any storms that were as strong and damaging as this last one?" asked Mark.

"Let's see. There have been quite a few dangerous hurricanes and Nor'easters over the years that caused extensive damage. But for us old-timers, that's the risk we're willing to take in order to live on this beautiful barrier island."

Mark pressed on. "But is there one storm that stands out?"

Dylan thought for a moment and then answered, "Yes. One storm that comes to mind. It was indeed a massive hurricane that struck during the summer of 1945. I remember it well.

"Back then, we didn't have early storm warning systems or long-range weather forecasts, which would have been helpful because that storm attacked like a frenzied pack of wolves that hadn't eaten for a week!"

Dylan's animated excitement caught the attention of the two boys. They quickly moved closer to their grandfather to listen since they had never heard of a storm described like that.

"Hey, Grandpa, what are you talking about?" asked Wayne.

"Ya see, that storm occurred toward the tail end of the Second World War. I only recall it so vividly because it hit with all of its might only one week after Christine and I purchased our house on Seventh Street. We were young and happy newlyweds!

"Your grandma and I had been painting the interior rooms of the house that day. We needed a break, so we decided to walk outside. That's when we realized that the beautiful morning had substantially changed."

Wayne asked, "What do you mean, Grandpa?"

"Well, we were really surprised at how the winds had become so fierce. More frightening were the coal-black clouds that quickly approached from the southeast, along with the rumble of thunder. In no time at all, the sky turned almost completely dark except for tremendous flashes of lightning.

Shaking his head, Dylan added, "Blame it on the paint fumes, but we were convinced that the damn Nazis had not surrendered, but instead Hitler had made some sort of pact with the Devil and was able to attack our country with a new kind of super storm weapon."

The boys intently listened to their grandfather as he said, "I have to admit, this likely sounds silly, but our imaginations were running wild at the time. In hindsight, after experiencing four long years of that frightful war against the Nazis, we likely weren't the only folks feeling the same way."

Dylan, looking a bit uncomfortable, adjusted his position in the boat seat. He then stared out over the ocean as if reflecting on long-forgotten memories before he continued. "Regardless, the storm hit Avalon like a blitzkrieg from every warplane in Germany's Luftwaffe air force. We experienced bullet-like hail, missile-like rain, tornado-like winds, and the biggest waves ever to hit Avalon. For two straight days, the entire island was ravaged by that storm!"

"How did you survive?" asked Wayne.

"Well, your grandma and I were very lucky. We took shelter in a large interior closet for most of it. Somehow, the house withstood the storm and had only minimal structural damage. Even so, Avalon lost a great deal of land and property. Amazingly, the storm deposited tons of earth and sand onto the northwest portion of our property. All said and done, we acquired almost two acres of new land, which essentially created our amazing lagoon!"

Mark then asked, "That's a lot of terrain. Was it yours to keep?"

Dylan responded, "Great question. I thought the same thing after the storm, especially since the elevation of the newly deposited land was several feet higher than our existing property. Fortunately, I worked with town and state officials and quickly reached an agreement to purchase a deed for the additional land and a grant for the water rights at a fair price. As a condition of the purchase, I agreed to immediately build a permanent bulkhead around the entire waterfront perimeter in order to ensure that the property would not erode back into the bay waters."

Dylan then went on to explain that he subsequently had his house lifted onto pilings so that it could sit at the same level as the newly acquired acreage. "While that storm was truly horrific in many ways, it improved our property. For that reason, I'll always remember that summer storm from 1945!"

As Dylan finished his story, Bob slowed his boat so that everyone could see the severe damage to the steel and concrete inlet bridge. The boys gazed in awe, contemplating how the extreme power of the recent storm had caused so much destruction.

As the boat headed eastward past the bridge, Wayne and Johnny moved to the front of the boat. The boys could not help but reflect on not only their grandfather's story but also the many other powerful storms that had struck Seven Mile

Island over the years. Johnny turned to Wayne and said, "It's really amazing how the island's residents are always willing to rebuild after big storms."

As the brothers looked over the boat's bow, they heard their dad's loud voice, "Boys, don't even think about hanging your legs over the sides! It's not only dangerous, but the marine police will arrest all of us if they spot legs extended over the boat's edge!"

While the boys had not dangled their feet over the bow, Johnny responded, "OK, Dad. Thanks for the reminder." The brothers then sat down, keeping a safe distance from the side.

"What's buggin' Dad?" said Wayne to his brother.

"Oh, you know how he gets when he's on a boat. Once a captain, always a captain! Anyways, how 'bout Grandpa's story? Awesome!"

The boys relaxed and enjoyed the rest of the boat ride as they continued to talk about storms, the Second World War, and how cool it was that Grandpa could so vividly remember such an amazing event that occurred forty years ago.

After exiting the inlet, Bob navigated the craft in a southbound direction, cruising about 250 yards parallel from the beach. The boat easily glided on the mild ocean swells as it passed by Seven Mile Island's large beaches on the right.

The adults discussed how the massive dunes just beyond the shoreline beaches had always been a blessing to the residents of Avalon and Stone Harbor. The hills of sand covered by dense vegetation and grasses provided a natural protective barrier from high ocean waves and the relentless series of storms.

"Just think of how much worse the damage might have been if not for those beautiful dunes," said Dylan. "I'm thankful that our local leaders understand the importance of maintaining the dunes and that they've enacted laws to ensure that the dunes will remain strong for years to come."

When they reached the island's southern tip, Bob turned the boat west into Hereford Inlet and then entered the Intracoastal Waterway. This well-marked, navigable body of water provided a smooth and safe path of travel through the bay waters. Bob followed the floating buoys and markers directly back to Grandpa's house at the northwestern tip of the island.

As the boat passed a green marker on its starboard side, Johnny turned to his brother and said, "It's cool how the buoys are really just like traffic signals, but for boats!"

Noticing another larger boat approaching on the waterway, Wayne added, "Yeah, the buoys prevent collisions with other boats and help captains from running aground in the shallow bay waters."

It was six o'clock when Bob pulled his boat into Dylan's lagoon to drop the group off at the Masters' bayside dock. Staring across the water, Bob remarked, "Hey, Dylan, it looks like you have some storm damage to your bulkhead. If you look on the other side of your lagoon, just beyond that large turtle, you can see the damage."

They all looked over at the tall wooden retaining wall that separated the bay waters from Dylan's property. Dylan acknowledged the appearance of a dislodged board and commented, "Hard to believe, but that's the original bulkhead I installed back in 1945. It's funny how one storm made me build the bulkhead, and now another storm is making me repair it!

"Tomorrow, I'll call a contractor and schedule someone to come out and estimate the cost of repairs."

Bob responded that he had a good friend who owned a seawall business. He added, "I'm certain that he can repair or replace the damaged bulkhead section for a reasonable price."

After Dylan got the contractor's name and number, they all thanked Bob for the boat ride and then headed inside.

That evening, the family relaxed. Everyone expressed how they loved spending quality time together. The boys mentioned that they especially enjoyed the boat cruise. After a light dinner, the family sat on the back deck and watched the sunset. A short time later, the boys said good night and went upstairs to the bedroom that they shared.

An hour after going to bed, Wayne sat up in the darkened room and asked, "Hey, are you awake? I just had a cool dream."

Johnny quickly responded, "Me too."

Wayne described his dream. "It was amazing. A German Luftwaffe airplane from World War Two was attacking Grandpa's house."

Johnny spun toward his brother. "I just had the same

dream! Wow, we sure were lucky that Grandpa, Dad, and Mr. Bloomfield protected us."

Johnny and Wayne described a truly amazing tale of how the three men used the boys' outdoor sporting collection of 1984 Olympic Games commemorative Frisbees to save the day.

The brothers had trouble controlling their laughter as they related how the men threw multiple Frisbees at the plane with uncanny speed and accuracy. Their fun tale came to a perfect climax when they agreed that every one of the discs miraculously struck their target, jamming the plane's steering flaps just before it could shoot at the house!

The boys loved exaggerating and embellishing each other's dreams. They always came up with "really cool" bedtime stories.

After several minutes of giggling and some excellent story-telling, the boys agreed that the disabled warplane was forced to retreat over the ocean and head back to Germany. Wayne then yawned and said, "Victory for the good guys!" Within seconds, both boys were sound asleep.

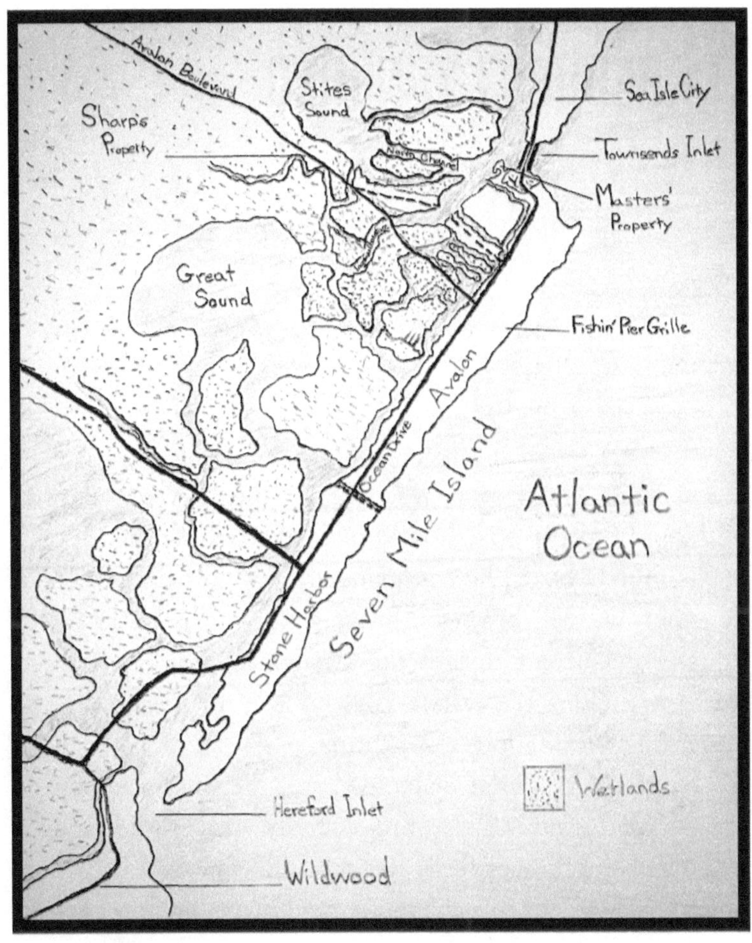

Avalon Boulevard
Sharp's Property
Stites Sound
Sea Isle City
Townsends Inlet
North Channel
Masters' Property
Great Sound
Fishin' Pier Grille
Ocean Drive
Avalon
Seven Mile Island
Atlantic Ocean
Stone Harbor
Wetlands
Hereford Inlet
Wildwood

CHAPTER 6
TORPEDOES LAUNCHED

{Atlantic Ocean – June 1945}

Twenty-four hours after reaching the Cape Verde Islands, Hitler ordered the vessels back to sea. Addressing the captains of the four U-boats, he commanded, "It's now time to leave. Together, we will head southwest along the Atlantic North Equatorial Current toward the Caribbean Sea. From there, we'll travel along the eastern coast of South America directly to our final destination in Argentina."

Interestingly, Hitler demanded that the vessels remain on the surface during this leg of the journey. At first, the captains welcomed the flow of fresh air and fully complied with their leaders' orders. But this changed when the sea became increasingly turbulent, and the bright blue skies turned menacing.

Captain Yeager was at the helm of the last U-boat in the convoy. With a concerned look, he turned to his lieutenant. "Schmidt, the weather is getting worse, and it is no longer safe to travel on the surface."

Franz Schmidt responded with a look of protest. "But, Captain, our Führer has ordered us to travel on the surface since the newly installed underwater radio transmitters are malfunctioning. If we submerge, we may lose contact and get separated. By remaining on the surface, at least we can still communicate with our backup VHF radios."

"May I remind you that I am the captain of this vessel, lieutenant commander! If we remain on the surface, this vessel will be in danger from not only the pending storm but also Allied airplanes and ships. Remember, the world believes that Germany has surrendered, and I'm certain that the Allied forces won't be happy to see four large U-boats heading toward the Americas!"

In an effort to avoid any further argument with the young officer, Captain Yeager headed to the radio room and transmitted his recommendations to the other three U-boats.

"My Führer, because of deteriorating weather conditions, I recommend that all U-boats submerge to a depth of twenty meters. Once leveled, we can continue to communicate with our backup two-way VHF radios by fully deploying our emergency antennas. By doing so, our convoy will not be impacted by the storm, and most respectfully, we can safely proceed in stealth mode, unobserved by any ships or planes." Yeager hoped that the Führer would be receptive to his suggestion, understanding that his U-boat captain was concerned for the safety of the German convoy.

Yeager soon realized that his message did not have the desired effect. In fact, Hitler was furious when he received the radio transmission. He shouted in an uncontrollable rage, "How dare you question my orders! This is treasonous!"

Unknown to Yeager or any of the other officers, Hitler was suffering from extreme motion sickness caused by the rough seas. As a result, he had become increasingly irrational.

Hitler commanded, "All U-boats will remain on the surface with hatches open! This is an order. If any captain disobeys, he will be immediately executed, and his vessel will be sunk!"

Upon hearing Hitler's directive over the radio, Lieutenant Commander Schmidt snapped at Yeager. "I warned you not to do anything to upset the Führer."

"I will not risk my life or the lives of my crew all because of his absurd order. Germany has lost the war. We must now save ourselves." Then, pointing up with alarm, Yeager cried out, "Look! Water is already coming through the hatch. This is madness!"

With that, Yeager turned to his highly skilled crew in the control room and ordered the hatch closed and the U-boat submerged.

Almost immediately, the other three U-boats began firing upon Yeager's submarine. Not surprisingly, Lieutenant Commander Schmidt was angry beyond control. He lunged at the captain in a frustrated attempt to gain control of the vessel. But Yeager was quick to react. He sidestepped the young officer's frontal attack and countered with a precisely thrown right-handed punch that struck Schmidt in the side of his head, just above his ear. The powerful blow knocked Franz to the floor of the control room, where he fell unconscious.

The next ten minutes were truly frightening for Yeager and his crew. While the three topside U-boats continued firing at Yeager's submerged craft, the strengthening storm had created large waves. As a result, they were unable to maintain stability, and their sophisticated weapons lost much of their accuracy.

After his vessel was jarred by a sudden impact that caused a frightening explosive sound, Yeager ordered his crew to return fire against the other U-boats. Holding his periscope with both hands, Yeager shouted, "Fire away!" At that moment, his XXI-A class submarine launched three torpedoes in defense.

Yeager alone witnessed direct hits to the three targets. While he did not see the U-boats sink, he knew that, at a minimum, each U-boat was impaired.

Over the next few minutes, the attack from the other U-boats subsided. Feeling relieved by the sudden calm, Yeager confirmed that his submarine was not significantly damaged. He then set a westward course and began to navigate his vessel away from the other U-boats. While holding the periscope in the control room, Yeager also began formulating a plan to surrender his U-boat to the Allies.

As Yeager wondered whether the other three XXI-A submarines would ever reach the new Fatherland, the unexpected happened. One of Hitler's damaged vessels successfully launched a long-range torpedo that struck the twin propellers at the rear of Yeager's U-boat.

A quick inspection by the crew confirmed that the sub's structure was not fatally compromised. Even so, Yeager's U-boat was suddenly adrift with no propulsion or navigation. Only the strong sea current and the increasingly powerful storm controlled their ultimate fate.

CHAPTER 7
SPECIAL GIFTS

{Avalon, NJ – June 1985}

Mark Sanders awoke at eight a.m. to his children's loud voices. Wayne and Johnny could be heard urging their sister to "hurry up" as they stood outside the upstairs bathroom door. Turning to face his wife, Mark rolled his eyes and smiled.

"Our kids are louder than any alarm clock!"

Liz sluggishly responded, "I wouldn't be surprised if they just woke up the entire island," as she buried her head under her pillow.

With the sun streaming through their bedroom window, Mark sensed it was going to be a very hot day. He followed his regular morning custom while at the shore; he headed downstairs and straight to the outdoor shower. He always enjoyed using the large private shower on the bayside of the house. Mark believed that the pulsating spray from the open-air ceiling was one of the real joys of the shore. He claimed that an outdoor rinse made him feel more alert and energized, whereas most islanders understood that outside showers were practical for washing away saltwater and beach sand. Either way, Mark definitely loved the outdoor shower.

Mark, Liz, and her parents had planned a surprise for the children that morning. The adults wanted the summer to begin on a high note, so they decided to give the kids a few special gifts that they would appreciate and use often while they were at the shore.

After breakfast, the adults presented Lisa with a brand-new Ross Signature road bicycle. Lisa was thrilled, yelling, "Thank you! Thank you! Thank you!" as she gave everyone heartfelt hugs. "This is just what I need to go back and forth to work this summer!"

The excitement did not stop there. The boys received Super Soaker 200 water guns and floating water polo goals. The boys were ecstatic!

Holding one of the Super Soakers high into the air, Johnny added, "Wow, this looks like it's from the new James Bond movie, *A View to a Kill*."

Wayne was even more excited about the water polo goals. While the entire family always enjoyed summer water polo games in the lagoon, the boys liked it so much, they joined a local competitive water polo team last fall. Of the two boys, Wayne was the more gifted athlete and he loved playing all kinds of sports, including swimming, surfing, waterskiing, volleyball, and soccer. But since starting league play, Wayne's favorite activity was definitely this fun action-packed aquatic team sport. Admiring the new goals, Wayne rejoiced, "Wow! This summer is going to be a blast!"

Johnny added, "These gifts are awesome." The boys then hugged their parents and grandparents as they shouted in unison, "Thank you!"

A short time later, Lisa rode her new red bike to her girl-friend Amy's house while Wayne and Johnny played outside with their new water guns. They had a blast pretending to be characters from the James Bond movie, and within no time at all, they were both drenched and very happy!

While the kids played with their latest prized possessions, Mark and Elizabeth sat on the back deck and quietly relaxed. Mark commented, "The kids really like their gifts. And your folks truly seem happy … and they look amazing too!"

Liz agreed. She told Mark how relieved she was that her parents' home did not sustain extensive damage from the latest storm, "other than the minor bulkhead damage."

The couple spent the rest of the afternoon together, simply mesmerized by the wonderful island views and weather.

That evening, Mark, Liz, and the boys walked from the house to Avalon's main business district on Dune Drive. As they passed the town's large pavilion at 21st Street, near the popular eatery, The Princeton, they observed Avalon's mayor speaking to a large gathering.

"As you all realize, our town has once again been hit by a significant storm, and some of you have suffered extensive damage to your homes and businesses. For anyone who does not have adequate insurance to cover your losses, please note that we are expecting to receive state and federal emergency aid. If you need assistance, please stop by the Municipal Building tomorrow morning with an itemized list of damages and repair estimates. We will have application forms for you to complete in order to be considered for the emergency aid."

Liz told Mark that she hadn't realized that the recent storm had caused so much damage on the island. "I really feel bad. Some of the islanders are really suffering."

As they continued walking, Mayor Carrington concluded his speech by saying, "While insurance may pay for some of the damages, and the government's aid will definitely help, the reality is that these funds still may not be enough to fix everything. With this in mind, the local American Legion Post has set up a collection table behind the pavilion where it is seeking donations for this good cause. If you are able, please contribute generously to help those in need as we take strides to restore our island community. Thank you, and have a nice evening."

Mark turned to his wife and said, "When we went on the boat ride yesterday, I was stunned by the extent of the damage to the bridge. And the significant damage to low-lying houses and buildings all around the island was upsetting. Let's make a donation."

Mark and Liz made a sizable donation and then continued their walk. A short time later, they stopped at the Paper Peddler bookstore, where Liz purchased a book written by the famous British author Jack Higgins. With the book *Confessional* in hand, Liz turned to her husband and said, "This is for Dad. You know how much he enjoys reading espionage novels!"

After leaving the store, Mark headed to the corner of 23rd and Dune Drive, which happened to be where the Avalon Freeze establishment was located. With a grin on his face, he said, "Who's up for ice cream?" He began laughing as the boys darted toward the shop's order window. The family always enjoyed the cool and delicious soft-serve cones while at the shore, especially on warm summer evenings.

Their final destination that evening was their favorite beach and toy store, Hoy's 5 & 10. After a quick visit to purchase two T-shirts for her sons, they returned to the house, where they relaxed in the large family room. Noticing that her two boys looked very tired and were both yawning, Liz said, "OK, boys, I think it's time for bed. Say good night." With that, everyone agreed that it had been a long day, and they headed to the upstairs bedrooms.

CHAPTER 8

TOSSED AND TURNED

{Atlantic Coastline – June 1945}

Yeager assessed the damages to his U-boat, and to his relief, he confirmed that the submarine's watertight hull was not breached. He and his crew then took measures to slowly guide the vessel up toward the ocean's surface. Even so, because of the direct strike to the sub's two propellers and rudder system, Yeager could no longer control his craft's direction or speed. Addressing his crew, Yeager announced, "We are fortunate that our vessel still has retained some battery functions. This will keep us buoyant and alive."

As the U-boat rose to within a few yards of the surface, Yeager used his periscope to search the horizon for any sign of his former convoy. Not speaking to anyone in particular, Yeager said, "I cannot see the other U-boats. We must keep our faith that we will soon drift to a port that will offer us sanctuary."

When Franz Schmidt finally regained consciousness, he began yelling at Yeager wildly. In response, Yeager ordered, "Confine this nuisance to the cargo room."

Franz was escorted out of the control room and placed in a previously locked storage compartment. The room offered very little space for Schmidt to maneuver since it was filled from floor to ceiling with an unbelievable number of cargo crates! Just before the door was closed and securely locked, Schmidt screamed at the top of his lungs, "You are a traitor, Captain Yeager!"

For the next two weeks, the rudderless XXI-A class U-boat was pushed by both the equatorial current and the massive storm system across the Atlantic. Captain Yeager estimated that his vessel was headed toward the Caribbean islands, where it would likely enter the warm and swift Gulf Stream waters.

As anticipated, the U-boat was carried past Florida and drifted northward, parallel to the eastern coast of the United States. Unfortunately, Yeager was truly distressed when several crewmembers passed away from severe injuries they had suffered during the recent attack on his U-boat. While alone in his quarters, the captain silently prayed for his rudderless vessel to quickly reach a safe port, as he did not want anyone else to be harmed.

Although the captain tried to maintain a positive and professional demeanor within the drifting U-boat, on June 20, his worst fears came true. Not only did the vessel's stern begin to leak, but the relentless tropical storm had turned into a very powerful hurricane!

Yeager's crew was helpless to do anything but hold on as the 130-mile-per-hour winds, torrential rain, and enormous ocean waves pushed the U-boat out of the Gulf Stream's grip and westward toward the shoreline.

In a brief moment of calm, Yeager climbed up the ladder that led to the conning tower and opened the U-boat's upper hatch. As he began to look to the horizon, a bright flash of lightning lit the sky. At that moment, Yeager witnessed a coastline less than a quarter mile to the west. For a fleeting moment, Yeager felt extraordinary relief, believing that he could now surrender his vessel and seek asylum in a friendly country.

Unfortunately for Yeager, his dreams were short-lived. Unexpectedly, a monstrous 125-foot-tall rogue wave came roaring from the east and crashed into the U-boat with astronomical power. The conning tower was instantly crushed, and the hatch torn from the vessel. With seawater pouring into the U-boat, there was little hope of saving the engulfed vessel.

The submarine was tossed and turned as if it were a small cork falling over a powerful waterfall. The great force of the wave carried the U-boat toward the shore, where it crashed into a large stone breakwater jetty that protruded from the coastline. At that moment, the U-boat suffered a fatal fracture and was propelled westward across the inundated island with unimaginable force. At the same time, Franz Schmidt was hurled out of the shattered cargo room and into the frenzied seawater.

The tsunamic wave ripped through the northeastern portion of Seven Mile Island, tearing up dozens of acres of beach dunes and shredding all that was in its path. Incomprehensible amounts of earth, sand, and debris were relocated and deposited over a half mile away at the island's northwestern side.

Life ceased that day for all occupants of the doomed U-boat except for one survivor. Somehow, Franz Schmidt managed to stay afloat as he was carried westward by the raging wave across the bay and through the North Channel.

Eventually, he was deposited onto a high section of marsh and sand located just south of Stites Sound.

CHAPTER 9
A NEW IDENTITY

{Seven Mile Island – June 1945}

For two days, Franz Schmidt remained unconscious, only to awake groggily to the distant sound of construction noises. With great difficulty, Franz sat up and began to focus on his surroundings of saltwater, aquatic plants, and high grasses.

While sitting in the middle of a vast wetland region, he quickly assessed that the activity came from the east since the sun was rising above a land formation just beyond a large body of water. He estimated that it was about a mile away. Then, peering to the south, he noticed a slight rise in the landscape about a quarter mile away. After assessing the area for several minutes, he concluded that it had to be some kind of narrow causeway or land bridge that cut directly through the wetlands, likely connecting two substantial landmasses.

Franz then made a decision to head toward the elevated land and somehow found the strength to navigate through the marshes. While trudging along, he began to recollect the recent events on the U-boat, including being thrown from the vessel, the turbulent waters, and a massive storm. After almost an hour, he finally reached the top of the land bridge, which was a narrow gravel-treated roadway.

Once standing on solid ground, Franz sighed in relief as he examined his own battered body. While he certainly was scraped and bruised by the ordeal, he was thankful that he had made it through with no significant injuries.

Without a plan, Franz simply turned toward the construction sounds and began walking. Because his shoes and most of his clothing had been stripped away by the force of the storm waves, Franz moved slowly and cautiously.

After a few minutes, he realized that he was extremely hungry. He ignored the feeling and focused on how grateful he was to be alive. He also started questioning his whereabouts. While he had no way of knowing, he hoped that he had landed in a friendly country.

As he continued walking, Franz noticed an abandoned pickup truck near the roadway. Though the truck's front end was buried in the marsh waters, the rear of the vehicle was still on dry land. It was then that he saw a silver Ford emblem displayed on the truck's tailgate, along with a tan license plate that read "N.J. 44." At that moment, Franz felt strongly that he was in the United States. He shook his head in amazement and uttered in English, "This must be America!"

Franz then reflected on his extensive military education and training in Germany. That was an optimistic time for the young German officer, who spent many hours mastering the English language. He had believed that learning to speak English would be very helpful as soon as Germany ruled England, Europe, and America. Deep in thought, Franz continued to walk slowly forward along the roadway.

A short time later, Franz noticed a small barn-like structure that sat along the south side of the causeway. It was just a few hundred yards west of a small bridge. As he approached the barn, Franz saw an elderly man struggling to lift several large boards out of a farm trailer. In a goodwill gesture to assist him, Franz rushed over and grabbed one end of the pile, helping to move the wood to the barn.

"Hey, thank you. I'm Sam Sharp, and I own Sharp's Fruits & Vegetables."

Franz responded in his best American-style English, "My pleasure, sir. Do you need more assistance?"

Sam wiped his brow, looked at Franz, and replied, "I sure do. But before I let you do anything more, I better get you some clothes. You look like you've had a rough time, young man."

Franz was quick to react. He explained in great detail how he had been working on a large fishing boat that was cruising along the coast. "We were not prepared for the storm's strength," he said in a dramatic manner. Franz then described how the large vessel had capsized, and somehow, he'd ended up in the surrounding marshland.

Sam felt badly for the battered fisherman. "You're lucky to be alive, young fella. Seven Mile Island was hit hard by that devilish storm! I was more fortunate. My property only suffered minimal damage compared with most others."

Franz thanked Sam for the clothing, and together, the men spent the rest of the day removing debris from the property and fixing several damaged sections of Sam's small barn and house. As they worked, Franz listened and learned. Sam talked continuously about his life in "the good old USA," and Franz quickly noted that Sam's business was located on the outskirts of Seven Mile Island, which Franz learned was one of New Jersey's southeastern coastal islands.

Sam continued, "Well, lad, my business may not be big,

but it's important to the local residents. Seven Mile Island has two towns, Avalon in the north and Stone Harbor in the south. And I have the pleasure of serving the best farm produce and fish to everyone!"

Pointing at the long causeway, Sam continued. "You see, my place is directly between the mainland and the island. That means that every vehicle that travels on the Boulevard must drive by here. I just try to make sure that I have plenty of fresh goods for all my customers.

Sam was grateful that Franz unexpectedly appeared that day. He thanked Franz with an offer. "Why don't you stay for dinner? And if you need a place to shack, I have a spare bedroom too."

That evening, Sam continued to talk about his small farm business and how he worked with several local fishermen and farmers to provide the island community with fresh fish, produce, dairy products, and general goods. He also talked about many of his island friends and described how he managed just fine even though he lived alone and had no living relatives.

As he listened to Sam, Franz devised a devious plan that would help him assimilate seamlessly into this rural island community. Recalling his years of military training, which included lengthy lessons on the topics of infiltration and reconnaissance, Franz coldly rationalized that he must kill the elderly man in the very near future! By doing so, he could easily assume the role of Sam's long-lost nephew, who came to the island to help his elderly uncle run the business. Franz reasoned that by temporarily filling this new role, he could easily search for the U-boat without raising anyone's suspicions. Once he located the sub, Franz believed that he could secure the valuable cargo and then find a way to continue his journey to Argentina, where he'd serve his Führer!

That night, Franz crept into Sam's bedroom as the older man slept. Silently standing next to the bed, Franz coldly forced a pillow down upon Sam's face and smothered his helpless victim. Deprived of oxygen, Sam unfairly died that night all because he welcomed the newcomer to his home.

Franz experienced no remorse. Instead, he justified his actions by believing that he was acting as a loyal servant of the Fatherland and the Führer. In a trancelike state, Franz obsessed, "To continue the Führer's mission, I'll survive by any means possible. I must find the U-boat, secure the cargo, and continue to Argentina!"

The next morning, Franz waved to a fire truck traveling along the causeway. Much to his surprise, the truck stopped, and the local fire chief yelled out the window, "Hi. I'm Chief Wilson. Just checking to see how you made out from the storm. Do you need any help of any kind?"

With some quick thinking, Franz fabricated a story about how he and his uncle had worked very hard the previous day to clean up the property, which sustained various damages from the storm. "By the way, I'm Sam's nephew, Frank Sharp. I'm staying with my uncle this summer, helping him run the business."

The fire chief exited his truck, and the two men shook hands. The chief then commented on how the storm had hit the area hard, noting, "Everyone's chipping in to help restore the island community. I actually just left the causeway bridge at 21st Street. We worked all night to unjam the swing draw-bridge. I was on my way to pick up supplies in Middle Township when I saw you wave. By the way, where's Sam this morning?"

"I think he's still in bed. I'll go check." Frank walked into the small house located behind the barn. A minute later, he cried out, "Chief Wilson, come quickly!"

The fire chief responded by running into the house, where he examined Sam Sharp in his bedroom. A few minutes later, the chief looked at Frank and said, "I'm truly sorry, son. This is just terrible. Your uncle has gone and died. The stress of the storm and working so hard yesterday seem to have gotten the best of him."

The chief called for an ambulance to transport Sam's body to the local funeral home. While waiting, the chief completed an accident report. He then asked Frank Sharp to read and sign the document since he was Sam's nephew and the only surviving relative.

Before driving away, the chief said, "I know this must be difficult for you. Old Sam was a good man. Please let me know if there is anything I can do."

From that day forward, Franz Schmidt was known only as Frank Sharp, the new owner of Sharp's Fruits & Vegetables. Because Frank claimed that all of his identification papers were lost in the storm, the sympathetic town and county officials assisted him with obtaining all new papers, easing the process of officially transferring the property to its new owner, Frank Sharp.

In the years that followed, Frank did a masterful job of hiding his true identity. He established himself as a competent businessman and a good neighbor to the island community. Even so, Frank Sharp could not rid himself of his unceasing quest to find the U-boat that had seemingly vanished with its golden cargo during the great storm!

CHAPTER 10
ANOTHER ACE

{Avalon, NJ – June 1985}

Lisa awoke on Monday morning in a great mood. She was really excited to be starting her new job at the Fishin' Pier Grille. Before she left for work her dad said, "I know that you'll do great, Lisa. Just be sure to smile a lot and use good manners. Who knows, it might help you to get some big tips!"

Together, they laughed, and Lisa replied, "Don't worry, Dad, I was already thinking the same thing."

As she rode off on her shiny new bicycle, she turned her head back toward the house and yelled to her father, "Love you!"

Meanwhile, the boys got an early start and headed to the 12th Street surfing beach. The previous evening, they saw a poster at the bookstore that advertised a volleyball tournament for boys and girls between the ages of 11 and 18 scheduled to start at nine a.m.

Fortunately for the boys, the walk to the beach was not very far. When they arrived at the round-robin tournament, Wayne and Johnny went to the registration tent, which was erected near the dune access path. The boys were told that each team comprised only two players. The brothers asked if they could be teammates and were happy when the official said, "That would be fine, boys."

During the course of the day, the brothers really had a blast. Wayne was the stronger athlete and performed exceptionally, and Johnny was spirited and used his good decision-making skills to keep pace.

"Wayne, it's your serve. We need two more points to reach twenty-one. You can do it."

With his brother's encouragement, Wayne tossed the ball high above his head with his left hand and then struck it hard with his firm right hand. It was a perfect strike as the ball elevated just over the almost eight-foot-tall net and landed on the sand court's right corner baseline. The referee signaled the point in favor of the boys.

"Awesome, Wayne! Serve another ace, and we'll make it to the finals," said Johnny. Wayne then launched a tremendous serve that landed inside the opponent's court without being touched by the diving defender. After the referee announced that the boys had won the game, Wayne and Johnny gave each other celebratory high-fives.

While elated to be moving on to the championship round, Johnny made a sensible suggestion to his brother. "Let's get something to drink and sit in the shade before the final game. We need to conserve our energy if we want to play our best."

Later that day, the boys performed even better in the final game. When the tournament concluded, the brother's vigor and energy had paid off. They were declared the winners of the 11- and 12-year-old age group. They also were awarded a fifty-dollar gift certificate from the tournament sponsors, the Avalon Anchorage Marina.

Both boys were extremely happy with their accomplishments. As they relaxed near the water, Johnny said, "I can't believe that we won."

Wayne replied with an exaggerated bravado, "Heck, those guys weren't so good. I bet if we enter all of the tournaments this summer, we'll be rich!"

Looking at each other in mock astonishment, the boys broke out laughing at Wayne's outrageous claim.

Prior to heading back to their grandparents' home, the boys walked along the beach towards Townsends Inlet. There they noticed an older man standing near the jetty that bordered the inlet. The man wore a yellow slicker that had Sharp's Fruits & Vegetables written on the back.

Wayne commented, "Wow, that guy has got to be hot wearing that slicker. It must be ninety degrees today!"

But Johnny noticed something different. "Hey, Wayne, check it out. That guy has a metal detector. I wonder if he's found anything cool now that the storm has churned everything up on the island. Who knows, maybe a piece of the bridge?"

"Well, I don't know about you, but I'm gonna ask him what he's looking for."

With excitement in their eyes, the boys ran over to the man. As they sprinted across the beach, Wayne added, "Who knows, maybe he's looking for pirate treasure!"

CHAPTER 11
GRANDPA'S STORIES

{Seven Mile Island – June 1985}

Walking through her parents' elegant dining room and into the large kitchen, Elizabeth looked at her watch and became alarmed that it was already 6:20 p.m. and the boys were not home yet. "Mark, do you think we should drive up to the beach to see what's keeping Johnny and Wayne?"

Mark, who was sitting out on the deck, held his right index finger up in the air in a gesture that communicated, "Just a second, Liz." At that very moment, he was enjoying ice-cold shrimp with cocktail sauce that Christine had just prepared. After wiping his face, he turned to his wife and responded, "Don't worry so much, Liz. The boys know that we are having dinner at seven. Let's give them a little more time to get home before we call in the cavalry for help." He then added with a big grin, "If the boys knew that we were having these wonderful shrimp as an appetizer, they definitely would have been home earlier."

As if on cue, the boys ran across the yard and up the porch steps onto the deck.

"Guess what?" Wayne yelled. "We won the volleyball tournament!" With huge smiles on their faces, the brothers started singing the chorus of one of their favorite songs, "We Are the Champions" by Queen.

The adults congratulated the boys and were pleasantly surprised to hear that Wayne and Johnny also won the gift certificate.

"That's really great, boys. Now, please hurry and wash up for dinner," said Mark.

Grandpa added, "I'm proud of you two. Wow, I wish I could have seen the action. What are you going to purchase with your prize voucher?"

From the main floor's powder room, Wayne replied, "Well, we're hoping to get a small trolling motor that we can hook up to your old dinghy, if that's OK, Grandpa?"

"That sounds like a great idea, boys. I'm happy that you want to use the rowboat this summer."

Johnny chimed in, "After our last game, we spoke to the tournament sponsor. He's a really nice guy who has run the Anchorage Marina for many years. He told us we could use the first prize certificate to eat at his marina's outdoor dining room, rent one of his small fishing boats, or even get some bait, tackle, or fuel.

"We told him that we planned to use your dinghy out in the bay this summer, and we were hoping to get a small trolling motor for it."

"Boy, were we glad when he told us that he had a slightly used trolling motor for sale that runs great and has enough power to easily propel the dinghy. While the gift certificate isn't enough to purchase the seventy-nine-dollar motor, he said that we could use it as a down payment. So, to buy the motor, we still need twenty-nine dollars."

Wayne told his family that he and his brother had two ideas for earning the additional money to pay for the motor. "Well, if we keep winning volleyball tournaments, then we're bound to get more gift certificates." With a shy smile, he added, "But we understand that we can't count on that."

Johnny then explained how they planned to earn money by catching crabs and selling them to Sharp's Fruits & Vegetables. "You see, after the tournament, we met another older guy on the beach, Mr. Sharp. He was searching for treasures with his metal detector. He told us that he owned the fruit and vegetable market on the causeway."

Wayne added, "That's right, Dad. He told us that if we catch blue crabs in the bay this summer, he'll pay us thirty cents for each crab as long as they are large and healthy. He sells them at his market. Johnny and I figure that by using the trolling motor, we can take the dinghy farther into the tidal marsh and catch a ton of crabs!"

As they continued talking about the day's excitement, the family members gathered around the large outdoor table for dinner. Before anyone ate, Grandpa said a short prayer. He not only gave thanks for the meal but also said how thankful he was to have the family together for the summer.

After everyone was situated with their plates of food, Mark addressed his sons. "OK, boys, I'll lend you the additional money for the motor. But I want you to pay me back. Also, we're going to purchase a first aid kit and an emergency flare for the boat because safety always comes first."

The boys eagerly agreed to their father's proposal, and then the excited brothers spoke about a boat safety class that they had completed earlier that month back at home. Specifically, they discussed how their instructor spent a great deal of time explaining the importance of having an emergency first aid kit on every boat.

Wayne added, "You just never know when an accident might occur, so it's better to be safe than sorry!" He then looked directly into his father's eyes and, with a slight smile on his face, said, "Johnny and I will definitely be safe on the dinghy. We have our boat safety certificates. Plus, we've spent our whole lives watching you out on your boat, and we've definitely learned from the best!"

Mark coughed in response to his son's exaggerated compliment, then simply responded, "OK, Wayne, it's time to eat your dinner."

As the family enjoyed their meal, Wayne asked Grandpa whether he knew Mr. Sharp.

"Yes, I know Frank. Actually, Christine and I met him shortly after we moved here. I guess it was sometime after the big storm that I mentioned earlier."

Johnny asked Grandpa if Mr. Sharp had ever found anything valuable with his metal detector.

"Heck, yes! Just last summer, I was sitting up on the beach reading a good book and enjoying life. Anyways, when I got home, I realized that my Seiko wristwatch was missing. Well, I knew that I had worn it to the beach, but I must have taken it off when I went for a swim. I immediately went back to look for it, but it was nowhere in sight. As I was about to leave, I saw Frank with his metal detector on the beach, and I explained my dilemma. Within no time at all, Frank located my watch in the sand. I was very grateful that Frank found it since it truly is one of my most treasured possessions."

Wayne said, "Really?" to which Grandpa explained, "Yes, it is. You see, your grandma gave me the watch as an anniversary gift a few years ago."

With that, Lisa said, "Wow, Mr. Sharp is a real treasure hunter!"

Wayne pressed further. "Wow, that's great that he helped you out, but do you know if Mr. Sharp has ever found anything really cool? You know, like chests filled with coins and jewelry, or even muskets and swords? You know what I mean, pirate stuff!"

Grandpa looked at the boys with amusement. Silently, he acknowledged that while his grandsons were very bright and mature at times, they still were just 12-year-old boys. He then responded, "As far as I know, Mr. Sharp has not yet struck it rich by treasure hunting. But it wouldn't surprise me if someday he finds something really valuable."

As the group finished their dinner, Lisa politely excused herself so that she and her girlfriend could walk to the nearby miniature golf venue on Dune Drive. After their long day at the beach, the boys were content staying put at their grandparents' home and eating delicious bowls of ice cream that Grandma had served them for dessert.

After cleaning the table and washing the dinner dishes, the adults and the boys relaxed on the back deck, where they enjoyed friendly conversation along with warm beverages.

Knowing that Johnny and Wayne were interested in Frank's treasure-hunting efforts, Grandpa addressed his grandsons. "Well, boys, did you know that New Jersey has had its fair share of pirate activity over the years? It's true."

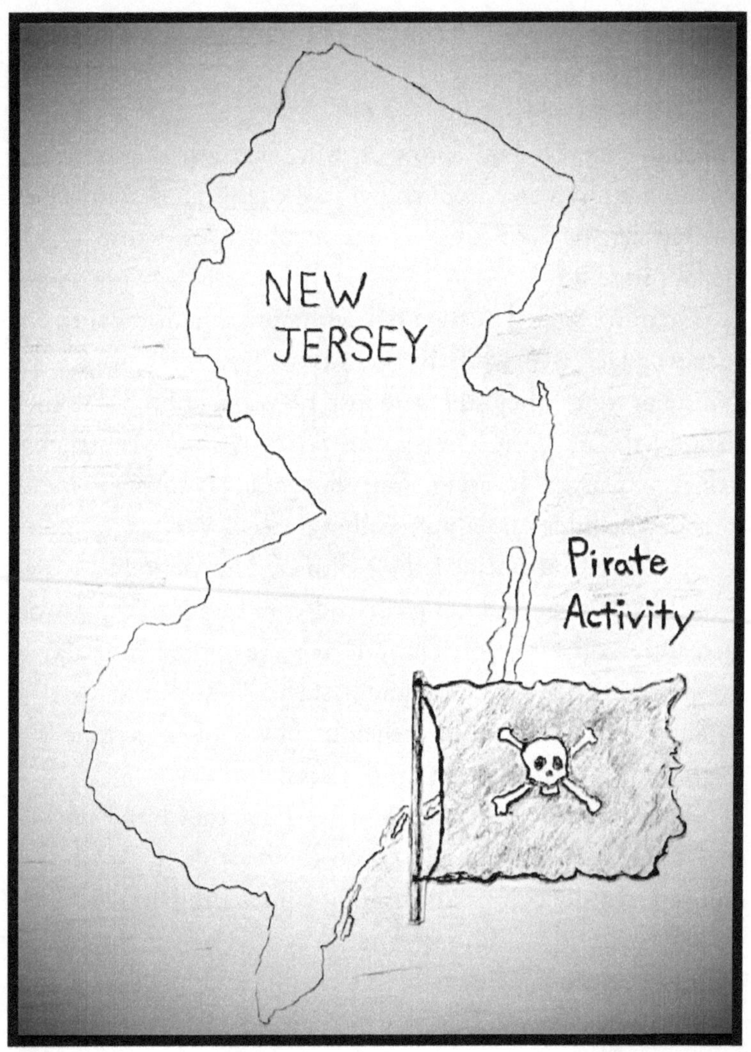

Grandpa then leaned closer. "I have several books on this topic. In fact, during the late 1600s, the infamous pirate Captain William Kidd was believed to have buried a huge treasure on one of the state's coastal islands. And another famous pirate named Edward Teach, also known as Black-beard, sailed the coastal waters of New Jersey around that time. Who knows, possibly both of these bandits buried their loot on Seven Mile Island!"

As the boys listened to their grandfather's words and continued to ask questions, it was obvious that Mark and Dylan really enjoyed the boys' excitement and curiosity on this stirring topic.

Grandpa then said, "Who knows, maybe Mr. Sharp is looking for war relics, too."

In response, Johnny asked, "What do you mean?"

Grandpa continued, "As we briefly discussed the other day, when I first met your grandma, our country was at war, and many Americans feared that warships and airplanes from Germany and Japan would invade our country."

Wayne interjected, "We learned about World War Two in history class last year."

Johnny jokingly corrected him by saying, "Well, at least I learned about the war!"

In response, Wayne gave him a firm push.

"Settle down, boys!" scolded Mark.

The boys quickly calmed down, knowing their parents did not like it when they argued or roughhoused in front of their grandparents.

Wayne said, "Our teacher told us that the war with Germany took place in Europe, and the war with Japan was in Asia and the Pacific islands."

Their grandfather leaned back and began to question the boys about the war. "I hope your teacher mentioned Pearl Harbor."

Johnny said, "Yes, we learned that it's on the island of Oahu, which is a part of the Hawaiian Islands in the Pacific Ocean. We spent several days discussing how Japan attacked the large US naval base at Pearl Harbor on December 7th, 1941."

Wayne added, "Hawaii wasn't a state yet, but it was one of our country's territories. After it was attacked by the Japanese, the United States was forced to enter the war."

"Well, I'm glad that you learned that important information," said Grandpa. "Did your teacher happen to mention how the Germans also attacked close to our shores?"

The boys said no, reacting with surprise.

Grandpa continued, "The Germans had a very advanced navy that included over a thousand submarines called U-boats. These frightening war machines wreaked havoc by traveling silently underwater. While submerged, the U-boats would fire torpedoes at enemy naval ships as well as neutral freight and passenger ships. For several years, Hitler's U-boats were truly just like pirates!

"I've always believed that Hitler was the most evil and deplorable of all pirates and that Germany's military was his own personal pirate ship. It seems that he wasn't satisfied with just ruling Germany. He wanted more. In my opinion, he was really just a monstrous bully who invaded his European neighbors at will. At first, the countries were frightened of 'Pirate Hitler.' But eventually, they just got fed up with him and decided to fight back. The really sad thing is that this evil pirate's actions caused enormous devastation, destruction, and death all over the world."

"Grandpa, are you talking about how the United States, England, and France fought Germany?" asked Johnny.

"Yes, those allied countries, along with many more. Initially, the US sent large cargo ships full of supplies to help our friends in Europe. Countries such as England and the Soviet Union were in desperate need of assistance. So, we sent them food, clothing, and military aid. But this was not enough to stop the Pirate Hitler. When he found out that the

US was helping his enemies, he ordered his U-boats into the Atlantic to destroy our convoys. In fact, on October 31st, 1941, one of his U-boats sank an American ship called the USS Reuben James. It was a destroyer that was guarding a convoy of supply vessels near Iceland. It was destroyed by just one German torpedo!"

Wayne seemed disgusted, and he asked, "Did this make Americans mad?"

Grandpa reflected. "Yes, but it also frightened many Americans. There was just no telling where or when the Germans would sink the next vessel. It was even reported that our ships were being sunk right off the eastern coast of the United States!"

"Was that why the US decided to go to war against Germany?" asked Johnny.

Grandpa gingerly said, "Well, it was certainly a strong factor in deciding whether to fight Pirate Hitler. People were upset that his U-boats roamed the seas like packs of wolves and then preyed on defenseless vessels."

Johnny persisted. "When did the US and Germany go to war?"

As Grandpa began discussing how Germany declared war on the United States several days after Japan bombed Pearl Harbor, Mark interrupted by saying, "Boys, I love the fact that you want to learn more about our country's history. But it's getting late, and it is now time for bed. Say good night."

Before the boys walked upstairs, Grandpa added, "Hey, just remember who won the war. You know, the good guys!" He smiled and added, "And boys, to answer your question about war relics here on Seven Mile Island, it's certainly a possibility. Back in 1942, we heard that just down the coast near Cape May, German U-boats sank 10 US merchant ships very close to the shoreline. In fact, debris from those wrecks littered the region's beaches for months. One fellow actually found one of the sunken ship's ring buoys that washed up on Avalon's beach! That's what I meant when I said that Mr. Sharp might also be searching for war relics here on the island."

Grandpa then told both boys that he loved them just before they ran upstairs to get ready for bed. He then turned to Mark and said, "Sorry for going on so long about the war. I hope that I haven't scared the boys."

"They'll be fine. Do you want another cup of coffee?"

As the men continued enjoying the peaceful evening, Mark asked, "Was there anything you could do here on the barrier islands to try to stop the U-boats?"

Dylan responded, "We did a number of things. First, there were mandated curfews all along the oceanfront communities. The coastal residents had to turn off their lights and radios at night because, during the war, many Atlantic ships relied on the lights and sounds from the beachfront towns to navigate at night. This included the Nazi U-boats! By leaving our lights and radios on, it made it easier for the subs to navigate the merchant shipping channels and then sink our ships. We hoped and prayed that our actions would prevent the U-boats from finding their targets."

"Was there anything else that you could do?" asked Mark.

"Well, the Civil Air Patrol flew airplanes and blimps up and down the coastline to try to locate U-boats."

Christine, who had remained contently quiet during the conversation, proudly spoke up. "Mark, did you know that Dylan was a volunteer Civil Air Patrol pilot here in New Jersey before we were married? His job was to search for enemy ships and U-boats!"

"Wow, you never told me that," expressed Mark with genuine respect and appreciation for Dylan's service. "Thanks for helping to protect our country, Dylan."

After Lisa came home, the adults finished their drinks, and everyone agreed that it was time to retire for the night.

CHAPTER 12
THE BIG GAP

{Avalon, NJ – June 1985}

Early the next morning, Lisa again headed off to work on her bike. The sun was rising as she crossed over Ocean Drive, the main thoroughfare that ran the island's entire length. This historic roadway, with its numerous bridges, was part of a fifty-mile span that connected the coastal islands scattered between Atlantic City, located to the north of Seven Mile Island, and Cape May, located at the southernmost point of New Jersey.

After zigzagging past the recreational park on 8th Street, Lisa turned right onto Avalon Avenue and headed toward the Community Hall located on 30th Street. She then locked her bicycle to the public bike rack outside the popular gathering place. From there, she walked a short distance on the town's oceanfront boardwalk and arrived at the Fishin' Pier Grille just as the front door opened. This small eatery was very popular with the local residents, as it offered delicious food, amazing views of the beach, and an ever-present island breeze that provided refreshing relief on hot summer days.

"Good morning, Lisa. Grab an apron and take care of those two customers," said the grille's owner. Much to Lisa's surprise, her two brothers stood by the front service counter with huge grins on their faces.

Wayne greeted his sister by saying, "Excuse me, ma'am, can we have a table with a good breeze?"

"Wow, what a surprise! I can't believe that you two got up this early." Johnny explained that Grandpa dropped them off since he was heading downtown for a Lions Club breakfast meeting that morning.

"Well, I'm happy to see you," said Lisa. "You are definitely my first customers today!" After introducing her brothers to her coworkers, Lisa walked the boys to a small table by an open window and took their orders.

"We'll have two large colas, two egg and cheese sandwiches, and two sticky buns, please!" said Wayne.

"Yeah, and if you're nice to us, we'll even give you a big tip," added Johnny.

With that, the three siblings laughed at the joke, then Lisa moved on to assist the other customers.

The boys not only loved their tasty breakfast but also enjoyed watching dozens of early risers walking and jogging along the boardwalk. When they finished eating, the boys said goodbye to their sister and started back to the house. As Lisa cleaned off their table, she could not help but think how impressive and surprising it was that her younger brothers had left her a tip. Reflecting for a moment, Lisa thought, "They're really not so bad."

When the boys arrived at their grandparents' house, they immediately put on their swimsuits and grabbed their water polo ball and caps, then headed to the large lagoon, where they placed the floating goals into the calm water.

The lagoon was protected on three sides by the bulkhead and dock. This formation unintentionally created a perfect saltwater playing field for the boys to practice their beloved aquatic sport without interference from the strong bay currents and waves.

At the Jersey Shore, the coastal waters rise and fall approximately every twelve hours, resulting in two high tides and two low tides each day. The changing water depth means that tidal waters are always on the move.

Over the next hour, the boys practiced passing and shooting the ball. They used their legs to perform the important eggbeater-style kicking motion, which enabled them to stay afloat and keep their heads high above the water's surface. They had learned the proper treading and throwing techniques at their spring practices back at home.

Recently, their water polo coach informed Mark and Liz that the boys had really improved throughout the season. He recommended that Wayne and Johnny continue training over the summer. "I'll be counting on the boys to help us win the league championship next season!"

While in the lagoon, Wayne said, "This sure beats homework!" He then swam using a modified front crawl stroke toward the floating goal, where Johnny was waiting to defend the net. As Wayne stroked, the ball floated between his arms and just in front of his chin. He quickly moved along the surface toward his target. When he was five yards in front of the goal, Wayne shouted, "Here it comes." He then scooped up the ball with his right hand and kicked simultaneously with his legs. This motion helped to raise his body well above the water's surface, enabling him to throw the ball with great speed at the net.

In response, Johnny reached to his left to try to block the rocketing ball. He was relieved when the ball hit the goalpost instead of his hand. The yellow ball then deflected toward the bulkhead, and the boys raced after it before suddenly stopping.

"Check it out," said Wayne as he pointed at a large turtle that was swimming next to the ball.

"Cool," said Johnny.

As the boys continued toward the ball, Wayne looked up and said, "Wow, look at the big gap in the wood," gesturing to the damaged bulkhead. "I guess this is what Mr. Bloomfield and Grandpa were talking about the other day. It looks like an entrance to a cave! I bet I can squeeze inside."

As Wayne tried to cram his body through the nine-inch-wide gap, Johnny opined, "You're too big, Wayne. We're gonna need Grandpa's crowbar to widen the entrance. Can you see anything inside?"

Wayne responded, "No, it's too dark, and the tide is too high. We can come back later when it's low tide. We'll need to bring the crowbar and a flashlight. Then we can really check out this cool cave!"

A short time later, Mark called out to the boys. "Let's go pick up the motor at the Avalon Anchorage Marina. We can be there and back in no time. It's at the end of 21st Street on the bay."

Within minutes, the boys and their dad drove to the marina. After parking on the side of the road, Mark asked his boys to look across the bay to a landmass located four hundred yards away.

"For over fifty years, there was a bridge that crossed the bay at this location," said Mark.

Johnny asked, "Where did it go?"

"About twenty years ago, the town leaders decided to dismantle the old 21st Street bridge since it was too small to handle the large volume of traffic. But not before the causeway was redirected and a new bridge was built at 30th Street."

Wayne responded, "Wow, Dad. You sure know a lot of stuff about the island. Uh, can we please get the trolling motor now?"

Mark and the boys then headed to the marina store, where they purchased the boat motor, first aid kit, and emergency flare.

After returning back to their grandparents' home, the

excited brothers expressed their sincere appreciation to their dad, who responded, "No problem. Now, you're ready to start crabbing. And if you do a good job, you can start your own crab charter business. But remember, the maximum capacity of the dinghy is three occupants. So only one paying customer at a time!"

The boys didn't think their dad's joke was funny. To them, this was serious business. Their goal was not to take any other passengers on the boat; rather, they aimed to catch as many crabs as possible so that they could sell them to Mr. Sharp.

Addressing his dad, Johnny said, "After we pay you back, we plan to put our earnings into the bank."

Wayne added, "And we're gonna use a little for having fun too!"

"OK, boys, that's great. I wish you all the best in your new crabbing business this summer."

The brothers truly believed that they were going to be successful crabbers even before their first crabbing venture. Fortunately, Grandma and Grandpa sat down with the boys and provided some important tips to ensure that their maiden voyage would be productive.

Grandpa instructed, "OK, boys. To be successful crabbers, you will need two basket traps, a large plastic bucket, crabbing nets, and hand lines with weighted clips."

Grandma added, with a secretive expression, "I'm also giving you two our top-secret bait recipe. We guarantee that this bait will attract many blue crabs into your nets." She then handed the boys a small plastic container filled with small chunks of chicken meat, hot dogs, and cat food!

After seeing the boys' looks of surprise, Grandma said, "Don't worry, your grandpa and I have been using this bait recipe for many years, and it has never failed!"

Grandpa continued, "The crabs generally like to hang out

in the shallow dark bay waters and near the muddy bottoms of the marshlands. After you catch the crabs, make certain to place them inside the empty bucket and lay a wet towel on top of the bucket to keep them cool and moist. They will still have ample air. Remember, Mr. Sharp won't purchase the crabs unless they are healthy and alive."

Johnny asked, "Shouldn't we fill the bucket with water so that the crabs can swim?"

Grandpa explained that if they did that, the crabs would quickly use up the oxygen in the water and would suffocate. The boys trusted their grandpa's advice and assured him that they would follow his instructions.

"Don't worry, Grandpa. We've got this under total control," said Wayne with a mischievous grin.

After a quick boat trip to a secluded area of marshland situated between Dylan's property and the Townsends Inlet Bridge, the boys entered a narrow channel that meandered into the marsh and began crabbing. Within two hours, the boys had successfully enticed fifteen large crabs to visit their bucket!

The excited boys returned to the house with their bucket of crabs. After thanking Grandma and Grandpa for their help, the boys asked their dad if he would drive them to Sharp's Fruits & Vegetables so they could sell their catch.

After greeting the boys and inspecting their crabs, Frank Sharp said, "Not bad, boys. At thirty cents per crab, I owe you $4.50."

Before departing, Mark commented, "Wait here, boys. I'll be just a minute. Your grandma asked me to pick up a few items for tonight's dinner." Mark then selected a dozen ears of fresh Jersey corn and several large tomatoes.

The brothers stood a few yards from the stand and talked about how they wanted to continue exploring the cave. Unknown to the boys, Frank Sharp was standing behind the nearby checkout table and overheard some of their comments.

This did not sit well with longtime customer Prudie Gray-stone, who wanted to pay for her selections. Noticing that Mr. Sharp was seemingly daydreaming, the elderly woman coughed loudly in an effort to get his attention. When he turned toward her, she quickly shoved her basket of fruits and vegetables into Frank's arms and said, "Well, it's about time, Mr. Sharp. I'm in a hurry!"

After returning to the Jeep, the boys gave their dad the money they earned, and Johnny said, "According to my calculations, we still owe you $24.50."

Mark thanked the boys for being responsible and added, "Nice job, guys."

Unfortunately for the boys, by the time they returned to the house, it was too late to go back into the water. Knowing that crabbing and swimming were done for the day, the boys decided to get things ready for exploring the cave the next day. After gathering their snorkel gear, waterproof flashlights, and two crowbars, Wayne said, "I'm starving. Let's see if dinner is ready."

Later, while in their bedroom, the boys discussed their plans for exploring the cave. After agreeing that they were prepared, the two exhausted brothers quickly fell asleep.

CHAPTER 13
FINS, MASKS, AND CRABS

{Seven Mile Island – June 1985}

Early the next morning, Grandpa received a telephone call from the contractor, Max Thomas. He advised Dylan that he couldn't make it to the house that day to inspect the damaged bulkhead.

"I'm really sorry, Dylan, but my team is still performing emergency work on the Stone Harbor Bridge. We discovered another issue that is taking longer than expected to fix. Once the work on the bridge is completed, I'll call you."

Although a little disappointed that the needed repairs to his bulkhead would be delayed, Grandpa responded, "Max, I fully understand that the safety of the island bridges takes priority over any needed repairs to my bulkhead. Be safe, and I'll wait for your call."

After breakfast, the boys headed out to the lagoon with their snorkel gear. They sat on the dock and slid their bare feet into the foot pockets of their swim fins. Then Wayne and

Johnny made a big production of spitting onto the glass lenses of their masks and rinsing them with water.

Grandma Masters was watching and asked, "Why did you spit into your masks?"

Johnny responded, "Sometimes the masks can fog up while in the water. When that happens, it's really hard to see. Last year, our swim coach told us that if we spit on the lenses of our swim goggles, they won't fog up. He also said that we should do the same thing when we use scuba masks!"

With a big smile, Wayne looked up at his grandmother, and with great bravado in his voice, he added, "Since then, we spit!"

Grandma broke out laughing as she thought Wayne's comment was hilarious, even if true. Before Grandma walked back to the house, she said, "Have fun, boys."

The boys entered the warm lagoon water and snorkeled toward the broken bulkhead. As they approached, they could see that the bay water was slowly entering the cavity located beyond the damaged bulkhead boards. After lifting their heads above the surface and removing their snorkels, they used their flashlights to look inside.

Wayne said, "I still can't see much, Johnny. Everything's just wet and dark. I think we've misjudged the tide 'cause the water's still way too deep."

The boys decided to wait a couple of hours for the tide to go down before trying again. Johnny proposed, "I really think we should try using the crowbar to widen the entrance."

As the boys swam back to the main dock, they optimistically plotted their next visit to what they now referred to as the "Pirate Cave"!

With their exploration plans on hold, the boys decided to go crabbing again. After talking to their grandfather, they agreed to head to the same place as their first outing, but this time, they would follow the channel deeper into the marsh to an area that Grandpa called the V-Pond.

Once on the bay, the dinghy headed northeast a short distance before turning into a small meandering channel. The boys followed it through the high marsh grass before reaching an open body of water that was shaped like the letter V. Although the saltwater pond measured only a couple hundred square feet, it was perfect for crabbing. There were plenty of dark, shallow areas where the boys effectively used their secret bait, along with their other crabbing gear, to catch thirty-two crabs in a little more than two hours!

"*Awesome!*" said Wayne as he admired their large catch. "That will give us $9.60 if Old Man Sharp likes our crabs. Quick, put the wet towel over the bucket! We have to get out of here before the tide gets too low and we get stuck."

The boys powered up the trolling motor and navigated the small craft out of the pond, through the channel, and toward the open bay. As they approached the channel's last bend before reaching the expansive bay waters, their motor sputtered, made a whining noise, and suddenly stopped! Johnny responded by quickly switching off the power to the motor. He then adjusted the small motor so that the propeller lifted above the shallow, muddy water. Looking over the rear stern of the small craft, he noticed that the propeller was entangled with a green fishing line.

The boys agreed that they needed to exit the boat and push it out of the channel toward the open bay. Johnny commented, "This really stinks. I wish fishermen would stop discarding their used fishing lines into the water. It causes so much damage. Not only to boats but also to the fish, turtles, and even the birds."

After entering the knee-deep muddy water, the boys easily pushed the boat around the bend of the canal and out of the marshland. They then guided the dinghy onto a sandbar that was exactly where the bay waters met the marsh.

Fortunately, Johnny had recently studied the instruction booklet that was included with the purchase of the trolling motor, and he fully understood how it worked. Turning to his brother, Johnny said, "No worries, Wayne. We have all the tools necessary to fix this mess right here in our gearbox."

After disconnecting the lightweight motor from the battery, they cut the visible fishing line with their utility knife and removed the line from the exterior of the propeller. Next, they loosened the prop nut with their wrench and removed the nut, washer, and propeller. Because there was no visible damage to the motor's shaft, the boys efficiently reassembled the motor in a short time.

After performing the emergency service, the boys placed the used fishing line into their trash bag and then decided to get wet. Together, they dove into the water that enveloped the small sandbar. Johnny rejoiced, "This is awesome!" Besides cooling off, the boys felt relieved to rinse off some of the sticky bug spray they had applied to their bodies before entering the marsh.

"I'm sure glad that Mom told us to pack the spray in the first aid kit. If not, we would have been eaten alive by those giant greenhead flies," said a relieved Wayne.

Once Wayne and Johnny were back at the house, Liz and Lisa agreed to take the boys directly to Sharp's market. After delivering their bucket of freshly caught crabs, Mr. Sharp said, "Boys, you are becoming two of the best crabbers on Seven Mile Island." He then complimented them on the large number of high quality crabs before adding with a big grin, "My customers really love eating crabs, so be sure to catch a lot more this summer!"

After thanking Mr. Sharp, the boys were even more elated when their mother treated them to delicious snow cones. They sat together at Sharp's large picnic table next to the barn and enjoyed the cold, thirst-quenching treat and the scenic views of the adjacent wetlands. Over the next few minutes, the kids told their mom about all of the exciting things that they were doing at the shore. Lisa described how much fun she was having at work and how she loved riding her new bike with her friends. Johnny then added that he was having a blast playing volleyball, riding waves at the beach, and swimming in the bay. Then, with grape syrup dripping all over his face, Wayne added, "I agree with you, Johnny. And we've also had a blast searching for buried pirate treasure."

Shaking her head in response to her son's imaginative comment about a treasure, Liz turned to her messy boys and said, "OK, my little treasure hunters, wipe your faces, and let's get going!"

As the family began moving toward their Jeep, Lisa noticed that Mr. Sharp was seemingly eavesdropping. Even so, she couldn't understand why he would want to listen to their small talk about snow cone flavors and how much she liked her new job.

When they returned back to the house at five o'clock, the boys went straight to their father and gave him the money that they earned that day.

"That's great, boys. Your debt is now reduced to $14.90. I'm really very proud of you two."

At that moment, Grandpa interjected by shouting, "Who wants to play water polo? Last one in the lagoon forfeits two goals."

In the following seconds, the entire family rushed to change into their bathing suits and ran out to the lagoon for a fun family game of water polo. One team consisted of Liz, Wayne, and Johnny, and the other team was made up of Dylan, Mark, and Lisa. Grandma assumed her regular role as the family's water polo referee. Wearing her favorite white hat and Polarized sunglasses, Grandma moved to her referee's chair located at the center of the dock. Gently swinging her official's whistle back and forth, she was happy to see her family so excited to play.

Dylan's team wore white water polo caps, and Liz's team wore blue caps. From the dock, Grandma shouted out, "All of you look more like sea turtles than athletes," referring to the cap's plastic protective ear covers. Everyone laughed at her joke, understanding that they did look kind of funny while swimming in the lagoon. Regardless, they had a wonderful time playing one of their favorite sports.

Liz and her sons really wanted revenge after losing so many times the previous summer. The boys were especially determined to play like Olympic champions, and they did. With Liz commanding, "Go long, Wayne" or "Pass it to Johnny," the team communicated well and played with perfection.

The men and Lisa simply could not keep up with the fierce aquatic speed of the boys. Dylan shockingly yelled, "Hey, Wayne, when did you learn to swim so fast and shoot so hard?"

After it was over, Grandma made the announcement. "The final score is 18 to 4, in favor of Liz and the boys. Way to go, Blue Team!"

After shaking hands, the family decided to celebrate on the back deck.

As he lounged on his favorite deck chair with a glass of cold lemonade, Grandpa looked out over the expansive bay and said, "This certainly is a wonderful way to celebrate." Then, turning to the others, he held his glass up in the air and toasted. "I really love all of you. Here's to a wonderful family and to Seven Mile Island!" to which Grandma added, "Hear, hear, Dylan."

That night, Grandpa ordered pizza from one of the island's favorite eateries, Circle Pizza. The family feasted on three large, thin-crusted pies covered with deliciously seasoned tomato sauce and mounds of mozzarella cheese.

In between mouthfuls of the tasty pizza, Wayne said, "Thanks, Grandpa. This is an awesome dinner. Mmm-Mmm Mighty Good!"

When the pizza was finished, and the dishes were cleared, the family gathered in the large family room to play a board game. Despite the normal debate concerning which game to select, everyone eventually agreed to try Scrabble.

The night belonged to Grandma and Grandpa, who won just about every round. Afterward, Dylan and Christine admitted that the game was stacked in their favor.

Dylan said, "Check it out," as he pointed up to a large trophy on top of a corner cabinet. It was engraved "1984

Avalon Yacht Club Scrabble Champions – Christine and Dylan Masters."

The kids definitely thought that the trophy was very cool, and they congratulated their grandparents on their accomplishment. Even so, Lisa also politely suggested, "If it's OK with you, maybe we should play a different game the next time."

Just before falling asleep that night, Wayne and Johnny agreed to continue their exploration of the Pirate Cave in the morning.

CHAPTER 14
THE SEARCH

{Avalon, NJ – June 1985}

The next morning, Dylan was sitting in his kitchen drinking a cup of coffee when the phone rang. Max Thomas greeted Dylan and explained that he was still working on the Stone Harbor Bridge. "The damage is worse than I originally thought. The wooden surface frames that surround the concrete pile driver supports were severely damaged by the storm. Unfortunately, it's going to take me another two days to complete the repairs."

Dylan indicated that he understood and then added, "Be safe, Max. I'm sure that everyone on the island truly appreciates your efforts to repair the bridge."

Knowing that his morning was now open, Dylan decided to head to the beach. After he changed into his swimsuit and walked downstairs, Liz called out.

"Oh, Dad, before you leave, I have a little gift for you that

I hope you'll enjoy." She handed him the new book that she recently purchased. "It's the latest by Jack Higgins."

With his spirits definitely on the rise, Dylan gave his daughter a hug and said, "That's so nice of you, Liz. Thank you." Then, grabbing his hat, beach badge, and beach chair, he left the house and happily began his trek.

After he left, Christine turned to her daughter and said, "Thanks, honey. Your dad really loves reading on the beach with his buddies. I'm certain that he'll enjoy the new book."

A short time later, the boys prepared to explore the cave again. At the same time, Mark and Liz sat on the back deck and discussed Mark's plans to drive back to Moorestown that day simply to check on their house and to make sure that the cat was OK. As they talked, their sons walked by and said that they were going to search the cave for pirate treasure.

Elizabeth responded, "That's great, boys, have fun," and Mark added, "Good hunting, boys."

Their parents were not paying attention to what the boys intended to do and did not see the items that they carried toward the dock. Johnny had two flashlights and the snorkel gear, and Wayne was carrying two large crowbars, which he had borrowed from his grandpa's garage. Had their parents been more observant, they certainly would have questioned the boys about the crowbars. And in all likelihood, Mark and Liz would have told the boys to stay away from the damaged bulkhead because it was dangerous!

The boys spent the next three hours in the lagoon. Fortunately, the tide was very low for a good deal of the time. Recently, in school, the boys' science teacher had explained that the normal monthly tide cycle was triggered by the full moon. That's when the moon, Earth, and sun are aligned, and the gravitational pull of the sun causes extreme tidal changes.

Because the tide was lower than normal, the boys could

stand on the sandy bottom with the waterline reaching only their waists. In turn, they felt more at ease while they worked.

Looking at the entire seawall, the boys understood that it was designed to hold the earth intact and to securely define their grandparents' waterfront property. The bulkhead was made of large wooden pilings with diameters similar to the size of telephone poles. The pilings were driven vertically into the ground every five feet along the wall. Behind the pilings were large wood boards called timber sheathings. One side of these boards faced the bay water, and the other side faced the dry land. The sheathings helped to hold the earth in place and prevented potential erosion of Dylan's property.

Progress was very slow and exhausting for Wayne and Johnny. But after much trial and error, the boys made headway by using the two crowbars to expand the gap between the two broken sheathing boards.

"All we have to do is move this board a few more inches to the right, and then we can squeeze inside," said Wayne with excitement. "By pulling at the same time, we can do it. On the count of three, give it everything you've got, Johnny! One. Two. Three!"

With all of their might, the boys pulled on their crowbars and forced the damaged board to finally move. Wiping sweat from his eyes, Johnny commented, "We did it. I think we can get into the cave now."

Before entering the enlarged gap, the boys took the crowbars back to the dock and returned with their flashlights. Unfortunately, because it took the boys several hours of hard work to expand the opening in the wall, the tide had changed, and the bay water was rising faster than anticipated. Even so, Wayne decided to enter the cave.

As he began to maneuver his body through the enlarged

gap, Wayne said, "We have just enough time for a quick look, Johnny."

His brother responded, "I'll stay just outside the cave entrance and keep my flashlight pointed at you at all times."

"OK, but if the pirates capture me, you better run for help."

Shaking his head in disbelief, Johnny lightly pushed Wayne in the arm and said, "Stop messing around, Wayne. We don't have much time."

Wayne easily negotiated his way through the small opening without scratching himself. Once inside the cave, he said, "Boy, this place stinks."

"What can you see?"

Wayne adjusted his flashlight and looked all around the dark cave. With the water now reaching his chest, he said, "All I can see are dark red and brown colors. I can't make out any details. The water's too deep."

As Wayne slowly directed his light toward the left, he saw a bright reflection. Unfortunately, it was only for a brief second and was seemingly doused by the rising tide.

Johnny urged his brother to hurry out of the cave. "Come on, Wayne, get out of there before the entrance is completely underwater!"

Once outside, Wayne said, "That was awesome, Johnny. We definitely have to check it out again at low tide. That's the only way we'll be able to find any treasure!"

As the brothers began to laugh, they heard their mom call, "Hurry up, boys. We're all going to The Princeton. It's Family Night and Uncle John's band is playing."

As the boys hurried out of the lagoon and back up to the house, Wayne said, "I love seeing The Snake Brothers band. Uncle John can really jam on his slide dobro and banjo. And that harmonica player is really amazing!"

"The whole band is great, Wayne. They not only sing well, but the fiddle, guitar, and bass players are the best."

When the boys reached the deck, Liz handed them towels and pointed to the outdoor shower. "Use soap and shampoo. You guys are a mess."

Before turning to enter the house, she gazed toward the marshland and thought about how beautiful Seven Mile Island was. With the sun setting, she noticed a tall egret walking at the water's edge while a group of ducks paddled nearby. "This place is amazing," she said to herself.

That night, the family had a blast tapping their feet to the beat of the lively music. The band played not only a wide range of popular rock songs but country western and bluegrass music too!

Christine convinced Dylan to get up and dance when Uncle John began singing one of her favorite songs from the 1960s, "Under the Boardwalk" by the Drifters. They continued dancing when the band started playing the next song, "Come a Little Bit Closer," which was a big hit for Jay and the Americans. With the band in full swing and spirits running high at The Princeton, numerous other guests joined the fun and began dancing.

As the brothers were watching the show, they noticed their grandparents dancing. After Grandpa spun his wife around in a full circle and the two ended the dance move with a quick kiss, the boys shouted in unison, "Yay, Grandma!"

Lisa followed by loudly yelling to Uncle John, "You rock, Uncle Ziggy," calling out his unique stage name. This caused Uncle John to laugh into his microphone while singing. A true professional, he quickly recovered without missing a beat and continued to serenade the crowd with a look of pure joy on his face.

When The Snake Brothers finished the show with an original song called "South Jersey Waltz", the family congratulated the bandmates for a terrific performance and headed back to the house. While walking with her family, Lisa silently reflected on a strange incident that had taken place that night. She'd noticed Mr. Sharp standing by himself on the other side of the dance floor. He'd done nothing unusual, but Lisa had felt a little uncomfortable because Mr. Sharp seemed to stare at her family's table for about fifteen minutes.

Thinking that he might just be shy or embarrassed to impose, Lisa thought it would be neighborly if she went over to greet Mr. Sharp. She walked across the crowded dance floor only to find that he had vanished. "Very strange," she thought.

As the family continued walking, Lisa could not help but reflect on Mr. Sharp's glaring eyes. The vision made her shiver from her head to her toes. Fortunately, her uncomfortable thoughts were broken when her dad walked over and placed his windbreaker over her shoulders.

"I saw you shaking and thought you might be cold. By the way, did you have fun tonight?"

"Thanks, Dad. I had a wonderful time, especially watching Grandma and Grandpa on the dance floor. They were great!"

But she didn't share her disturbing thoughts about Mr. Sharp and his glaring eyes.

CHAPTER 15
"I COULD USE A LITTLE HELP"

{Seven Mile Island – June 1985}

"Hey, Johnny, wake up. I just checked with Grandpa, and he said it's a perfect time to go crabbing. I bet if we leave now, we'll catch a ton of crabs. Then we can earn enough to square up with Dad."

Johnny responded by throwing his pillow at Wayne and moaning, "Why did you wake me up so early? Let me sleep."

Wayne certainly was not going to let that happen. Instead, he dove onto Johnny's bed, pinning him down while tickling him. After a minute, Johnny managed to slide off the bed and scramble downstairs with Wayne in hot pursuit.

After their mom promptly stopped the chase, the two boys settled down and then sat with their grandparents at the kitchen table for breakfast. While eating, the boys planned another day of crabbing.

"Let's try that other place Grandpa mentioned," Wayne

said. "You remember the place on the west side of the bay called Stites Sound. Grandpa said it's a great place to crab."

Grandpa chimed in. "That's right, boys, I've caught a ton of crabs at the sound over the years. Just be sure to stay close to the high grass areas."

A short time later, the boys motored the dinghy across the quiet bay and into the North Channel. From there, the vessel entered a small canal and slowly cruised through the wetlands toward the promising crabbing site.

Their grandfather had been correct. The crabbing was fantastic that morning!

"I'm really glad that we brought two buckets with us," said Johnny. "I can't believe that we just caught forty crabs. If Mr. Sharp likes them, we'll earn another twelve dollars."

Feeling good about their successful crabbing trip, Johnny steered the boat out of the wetlands. As they approached the bay, Wayne said, "The wind has really picked up, and the water's getting choppy." Sitting at the stern, Johnny glanced at the surprisingly powerful motor and responded, "You have to admit, this sure is easier than using the oars!"

Halfway back to the house, Wayne said, "Guess where we might go tonight?"

"Where?"

Wayne recounted how he overheard his parents talking about taking everyone to the two amusement park piers in Wildwood.

"That's awesome!" said Johnny. Then, he excitedly talked of how much he enjoyed visiting this neighboring barrier island, which is just south of Seven Mile Island. Especially because Johnny loved riding on roller coasters. "Hey, maybe we can ride the Golden Nugget Mine Ride or The Flyer roller coaster at Hunt's Pier. And if we have time, let's try the Sea

Serpent roller coaster at Morey's Piers. I heard that it's awesome!"

As they continued back toward their grandparents' home, Wayne reminded his brother of all the fantastic food at the amusement park. "Maybe we can get some pizza, or fries, or even funnel cake! And if we're still hungry, we can share a giant bag of saltwater taffy and some cotton candy."

Johnny just shook his head and laughed. "You're crazy, Wayne. You can eat anytime. But tonight, roller coasters rule!"

After the boys docked the boat and unloaded, Liz and Lisa drove them to the Sharp's Fruits & Vegetables stand to sell their catch. Frank was in a very good mood and happily purchased the shellfish from the boys. Frank asked the boys, "Are you having a good summer with your grandparents?" The brothers answered by telling Mr. Sharp that they were having a great time. They then described how they were playing volleyball games, going out in their dinghy, playing water polo, and using their water guns.

As an afterthought, Johnny added, "And we are also having fun being treasure hunters just like you!"

Almost immediately, Frank's disposition became less friendly. He suddenly turned away and muttered, "Oh, well, ah, have fun, boys."

On the drive back to the house, Lisa expressed surprise at how quickly Mr. Sharp brushed off the boys after being so nice when they first arrived.

Elizabeth calmly said, "Mr. Sharp has a business to run and doesn't have much time to talk to kids. Think about it, honey, he had other customers. How long do you get to talk with people while waiting at the Fishin' Pier Grille?"

Lisa lowered her head and replied, "I guess you're right, Mom. Sorry."

When the boys exited the Jeep back at the house, they noticed that the tide was low. "Mom, is it OK if we go swimming in the lagoon?"

Liz responded, "That's fine, boys. But we're all going to Wildwood in an hour, so I want you out of the water in forty-five minutes so you can get cleaned up before we leave. You're not wearing wet swimsuits to the amusement park!"

In a flash, Johnny and Wayne hurried out to the lagoon with their gear bag filled with their fins, masks, and flashlights. After snorkeling through the water to the enlarged crevice, Wayne reentered the dark hollow den and said, "Wow, this cave smells even worse today. It's like a backed-up toilet!"

Johnny followed his brother through the hole and had a look of disbelief as he expressed, "You're not kidding. This place is really creepy. There's slime everywhere!"

As Wayne moved deeper into the gloomy interior, he said, "Johnny, look over here. Aim your flashlight where my light is shining. Do you see that small bright spot?"

Johnny directed his light in the same direction. "Yeah, I see it. Is it a turtle shell?"

Wayne said that he didn't think so. "Let me take a closer look. Keep shining your light on it."

Wayne then moved toward the unknown object in the wet cavern. After bumping into multiple submerged objects, he handed his flashlight to his brother and then attempted to grab the object. "This thing sure is heavy. Whatever it is, it's slippery too! I can't get a firm grip on it."

Turning back toward his brother, Wayne commanded, "Come here, Johnny. I need your help lifting this thing." After navigating toward Wayne, Johnny evaluated the situation and decided that the easiest way to move their discovery outside the cave would be to place the odd rectangular object into their gear bag. By doing so, they wouldn't risk dropping or losing the slippery object.

With great effort, the boys successfully placed it into the duffle bag.

Johnny was surprised by the object's weight and exclaimed, "You're right. This thing is heavy. It must weigh thirty pounds!"

As they worked their way back toward the opening of the cavern, the bag handle slipped from Johnny's grasp, and the loaded bag quickly dropped several feet to the bottom of the cave.

With frustration in his voice, Johnny said, "Sorry, Wayne!"

Without hesitation, Wayne went below the surface, and a few seconds later, he came up coughing. "I've got it," he croaked while tightly gripping the bag handles. With Johnny's bright flashlight shining into his eyes, Wayne muttered, "Hey, turn that thing away from my eyes. You're blinding me!" He then coughed again and added, "I could use a little help."

Together, the boys carried the heavy bag to the cave's opening and shoved it through the parted boards. After exiting, they carried the bag and their gear through waist-deep water directly to the boat dock about twenty yards away. Just as the anxious brothers lifted their find onto the dry dock, they heard their mom yell, "Boys, we are leaving for Wildwood in two minutes. Get up here now!"

With that, the boys scrambled up the dock's wooden ladder and promptly maneuvered the gear bag into the dock's storage chest bench. As they dashed toward the outdoor shower, Wayne said, "We better hurry before Mom decides to call off the trip to the amusement park!"

CHAPTER 16
AMUSEMENT PARK FUN

{Wildwood, NJ – June 1985}

A short time later, the family arrived at the popular resort destination of Wildwood. Knowing that they had only a few hours, the family headed straight toward the beach, where a massive boardwalk ran parallel to the ocean.

The boys were visibly excited as they approached Morey's Piers Amusement Park. The entertainment complex was situated on two large wooden piers that extended east from the main boardwalk, over the beach, directly to the surf line. Instead of being a landing stage for boats and ships, these piers were used solely to accommodate dozens of incredible and exciting amusement thrill rides and games.

While walking along the boardwalk, they enjoyed looking out at the expansive beach to the east and at the stores, restaurants, and arcade booths to the west. Before the kids entered the park area, Grandpa treated everyone to a fun summer meal consisting of lemonade, wings, fries, and funnel cakes at the popular eatery called Curley's.

"Kids, you just set a speed record for eating!" said Mark.

"But Dad, we don't have much time to go on the amusement rides," said Wayne.

With that, Mark responded, "Relax, you have three hours to enjoy the rides. Just remember, we are meeting at the Ferris wheel at nine-thirty sharp!"

Wayne, Johnny, Lisa, and Amy then darted off toward the amusement rides while the adults talked about checking out the numerous stores on the boardwalk.

A moment later, Liz turned to her husband and parents and said, "I'd actually like to ride the giant Ferris wheel. Any takers?"

"That's a marvelous idea!" replied Grandpa as he immediately began walking toward the popular ride.

That evening, the kids had a terrific time riding both traditional-style and boomerang-style roller coasters. They also enjoyed colliding into one another on the popular bumper cars and couldn't stop laughing as they walked through the fun house.

As the girls climbed off one of the cool rides, Lisa was caught by surprise when her girlfriend Amy said, "Lisa, your brothers are kind of cute. Wayne's really funny, too!"

Not knowing what to say, Lisa blurted, "Uhhh, uhhh, thanks." Then, she quickly changed the subject. "Hey, we only have fifteen minutes before we have to meet Mom and Dad at the Ferris wheel. There's just enough time to ride the Sea Serpent. Let's hurry!"

"Great, you're right on time," said Grandpa as he smiled at the kids.

"Let's head back to my van."

As the family began the trek away from the rides, the kids agreed that it was a really fun evening.

"Thanks again for inviting me to the park, Lisa," said Amy.

"The steep drop on the Sea Serpent was awesome, especially when those crazy blinking lights blinded us just before the final turn!"

"I hope I didn't hurt your ears too much when I screamed, Wayne."

"Are you kidding me?" Wayne said in disbelief.

"Everybody was screaming. That ride was absolutely amazing!"

Johnny and Lisa agreed that it was definitely the best ride of the evening.

As they strolled away from the rides, Mark commented, "I really had fun tonight. The views from the top of the Ferris wheel were unbelievable! The only thing that I really didn't care for were those annoying tramcars. I almost got clobbered by one that was driving way too fast! And the driver just looked at me and laughed when I had to jump out of his way!"

Christine responded, "Hey, Mark. Be nice! Dylan and I enjoyed our tramcar ride. They help to transport folks up and down the boardwalk. Plus, it's much easier than walking!"

Liz laughed as she turned to her husband and whispered into his ear, "She certainly told you, Mr. Opinionated!"

A few moments later, the boys managed to convince their dad to splurge on cotton candy. While the kids enjoyed one last treat at the park, Grandpa mused, "I can't believe how loud the park has gotten. It wasn't so loud ten years ago." Mark and Liz looked at each other and knowingly smiled before Liz patiently said, "You're probably right, Dad. Thanks again for driving tonight."

After dropping Amy off at her house, the family arrived home at 10:45 p.m. While everyone was heading for bed, Lisa told her parents, "I think I'm going to sit out back on the deck for a few minutes. The stars really look incredible tonight."

"No problem, honey," said Mark, "but you probably won't be able to see the stars for much longer. Grandpa told me that we're supposed to get some heavy fog tonight. And remember, you have to work tomorrow morning! So don't stay up too late."

CHAPTER 17
KIDNAPPED

{Seven Mile Island – June 1985}

While sitting on a comfortable chaise lounge chair with her legs extended toward the calm bay water, Lisa stared up at the night sky and reflected on how much fun she was having at the shore. She really liked her new job and thought it was a great way to earn a few dollars while meeting people her own age. She also thought about what Amy had said about Wayne and Johnny earlier that evening. Much to her surprise, Lisa had to admit that her brothers had been pretty cool since they'd all arrived at the shore.

As she relaxed, Lisa sensed movement in the shadows near the dock. She stood up and walked toward the lagoon. "Hey, who's there?"

All at once, a blurred figure jumped up from the dock's ladder and roughly grabbed the startled teenager. The anonymous person, who was dressed from head to toe in black clothing, acted with speed and strength. The only thing that Lisa could manage to do was scream, "Help! Help!"

Almost immediately, the intruder put a gloved hand over her mouth and commanded, "Shut up!" Those were the only words Lisa heard before the assailant threw her into a small powerboat a few feet away in the lagoon. Striking her head on the side of the boat's interior wall, Lisa thought of her family as she slipped into unconsciousness.

At that same moment, Wayne stirred restlessly in his bed. His inability to sleep was likely due to the large portion of fluffy sugar-spun cotton candy he ate before leaving Wildwood.

When Wayne heard the sound of a scream through the

open bedroom window, he sat up and urgently said, "Johnny, did you hear that noise?"

Johnny, who was also having difficulty sleeping, sprang up and said, "Yeah. It sounded like Lisa. Let's check it out!"

The boys quickly peered out the side-by-side double-hung window and witnessed a large dark figure at the water's edge push their sister into a boat. Immediately, the boys yelled for their dad and darted into the hallway.

Seeing their father, Johnny blurted out, "Dad, Lisa's in trouble! We heard her scream and saw someone throw her off the dock into a powerboat!"

The boys never saw their father react so quickly. In a flash, he was down the stairs and out the back door, running toward the lagoon. Not missing a beat, Wayne and Johnny quickly pursued their dad outside.

By the time Mark and his sons reached the dock, Lisa was missing. Looking out over the bay, they witnessed the small speedboat rapidly accelerate away from the lagoon.

Seeing his wife walk out onto the back deck, Mark yelled, "Liz, call the police! I think someone's taken Lisa!" He then hurried toward his Boston Whaler and shouted, "I'm going after that boat. It's headed south in the bay!"

Before he boarded his craft, Liz yelled back, "Take the boys with you. They can use your floodlights to help track the other boat. And please be careful." She then dashed into the house, where she immediately called the Avalon Police Department.

Mark swiftly untied the boat lines, then jumped into the captain's chair at the center console and started the engine. After switching on the boat's running lights, which helped to illuminate the vessel at night, he made certain that the boys were safely seated on the custom bench positioned directly in front of the operating console. "OK, boys, let's roll." Mark advanced the throttle as far as it could go, and the Whaler rocketed out of its boat slip and headed directly into the dark bay waters in hot pursuit of the mystery powerboat.

As a former naval officer, Mark was a skilled and competent boat operator. Because of this, he could be demanding of Wayne and Johnny when it came to boating.

As Mark maneuvered the craft into open waters, he shouted above the loud roar of the engine for the boys to grab the two floodlights.

"Johnny, aim your floodlight into the water just beyond the bow of our boat! Wayne, aim your light at the other boat!"

With a half-mile head start, the fleeing vessel swiftly moved south through the Ingram Thorofare channel without using any running lights. Fortunately, Wayne spotted the unidentified boat's trailing wake waves in the eerily dark water, which allowed Mark to more easily pursue the escaping craft.

Because Mark's boat had a powerful engine, he was able to gain on the vessel. After just a few minutes, Johnny yelled, "We're catching up, Dad!"

With the lead boat more visible, Mark and the boys saw the craft suddenly slow to a crawl as it approached the large Avalon Boulevard Bridge. Because the bridge lights illuminated the surroundings, Mark saw the boat operator push something large into the water. Then, the powerboat quickly disappeared into the darkness underneath the bridge.

With the boys' floodlights guiding the way, Mark immediately recognized his daughter waving her arms from the surface of the water. He reduced the Whaler's speed and told Johnny to remain in his seat and to keep his light aimed at Lisa.

After Mark skillfully guided the boat alongside Lisa,

Wayne took quick action by extending a personal floatation cushion to his sister. "Grab ahold. I'll pull you in." He then helped his sister climb up the side gunwale ladder and into the vessel.

"Oh my God! You saved me," cried Lisa as she collapsed into Wayne's arms. Not to miss a beat, Johnny was there with a large beach towel that he grabbed from the storage bin in the front bow. While wrapping it around Lisa, he comforted her. "You're safe now, sis. Everything's OK."

After making certain that Lisa was not seriously injured, Mark used the boat's VHF radio microphone to transmit a message to the marine police. "Mayday, mayday. This is Mark Sanders calling the Avalon Marine Patrol."

After receiving a prompt response, Mark explained their situation and location. The dispatcher told Mark to remain there as a patrol boat was on its way. Because a dense fog was coming on, Mark launched a red distress flare high into the night sky, hoping it would help the police to pinpoint their position.

While Mark and the boys were rescuing Lisa, the kidnapper's speedboat seemingly vanished without a trace. As much as Mark would have liked to identify the kidnapper, he was more than satisfied knowing that Lisa was out of danger. And he understood that it would not be wise to continue the pursuit since the dense fog was now enveloping his boat, and he did not want to take any risks with his children on board.

Without delay, the police boat reached the Whaler. After checking to make sure that Lisa was comfortable and not visibly harmed, the marine patrolman instructed Mark to follow him to the Avalon public marina. A short time later, the two vessels pulled into the marina and docked at two vacant boat slips. After the Sanders family disembarked, a large police motor vehicle transported everyone to the nearby headquarters for questioning.

The next few hours were fueled with anxiety, fear, relief, and multiple cups of warm cocoa and coffee. Lisa was frustrated because she was unable to provide the police detective with meaningful details about her kidnapper or the assailant's boat. She recalled only that the assailant was dressed in black. When asked to describe the attacker's voice, she said, "I'm sorry, but I can't remember. Everything's a blur."

Lisa described one detail that had the potential to help the police. "After I woke up on the boat, I remember my head hurting. Then the engine noise wasn't so loud. That's when someone lifted me. As I was being pushed toward the side of the boat, I think I scratched the person with my right fingers. I could feel my nails scraping skin before they got caught on something. I'm not positive, but it may have been a glove. That's when I splashed into the water."

The detective asked her to try to remember if she pulled the glove off. Lisa said, "I'm really not sure. My fingers snapped back just before I landed in the bay."

As the questioning continued, Lisa was relieved when her mom and grandpa walked into the station. "Oh, honey! Are you OK?" Liz ran to hug her daughter.

"I'm feeling better, Mom. Though I don't understand how this could happen. Why me?"

As part of his investigation, the detective began taking detailed photographs and measurements of Lisa's right hand and fingernails. He also secured nail scrape samples and sealed them in a specimen container.

The detective explained, "By documenting this evidence, the forensic experts at the state police laboratory in Hammonton might be able to find information that will help us to identify the assailant. And if we locate a suspect, we can compare any wound markings with the measurements and dimensions of your hand, fingers, and nails."

While the detective was speaking with Lisa, Grandpa asked his old friend Chief Grant, "Would it be all right if we ask Dr. Craig Mitchell to stop by to take a look at Lisa?"

Liz added, "We truly would appreciate it, Chief."

Knowing that Dr. Mitchell was Dylan and Christine's family physician and resided nearby, the chief responded, "That's a good idea, Dylan. I'll give him a call."

A few minutes later, Dr. Mitchell walked into the station. After examining Lisa, he spoke privately to Liz and Mark.

"Considering the extraordinary events of the past few hours, I believe that Lisa is really holding up well. While she has a few minor bruises, overall, her physical and mental states are remarkably good."

With a concerned expression on her face, Liz asked, "Dr. Mitchell, will Lisa be OK?"

"Because she suffered a blow to her head and lost consciousness briefly, there is a chance that she has suffered a mild concussion. With this in mind, Lisa should get some rest and refrain from physical activities for a few days. If she experiences headaches, fatigue, blurred vision, disorientation, or nausea, please call me immediately for a more thorough examination."

He optimistically added, "With that said, your daughter appears to be a healthy young lady, and she is not showing any signs of a concussion at this time. I'm sure that with some rest and with the love of her family, there's a very good chance that she'll be just fine."

After the doctor left the station, Chief Grant told the family that he would keep them informed as to his investigation. Grandpa then drove Liz, Lisa, and the boys back to the house, and the chief took Mark back to the marina so that he could retrieve his boat. After thanking Chief Grant, Mark promptly navigated his Whaler back to Dylan's dock.

Before climbing the stairs to her bedroom, Lisa asked her mom to call the Fishin' Pier Grille to let the owner know that she wouldn't make it to work after her traumatic night. Stopping halfway up the stairs, Lisa looked out the large window toward the inlet and witnessed a stunning sunrise over the Atlantic Ocean. She whispered to no one in particular, "That's so beautiful," before heading to her bedroom.

Later that morning, the adults sat around the kitchen table and processed what had happened. They could not fathom why anyone would want to kidnap Lisa. The more they thought about it, the more frustrated they became. The situation was made even worse with their knowing that the police didn't yet have leads to investigate.

In an effort to raise everyone's spirits, Elizabeth said, "Well, if I had to guess, I think it was likely one of the boys I saw flirting with Lisa and Amy at the beach. Maybe it was a stupid, mischievous prank that got way out of hand. I can't imagine he meant to scare her like he did."

Although the others all nodded as if they agreed with Liz, deep in their hearts, they all had their doubts.

CHAPTER 18
THE ESCAPE

After purposely slowing his boat as he neared the well-lit bridge, Frank Sharp pushed the startled girl into the water and then sped off into the darkness. He traveled south for a short distance before turning west into a small camouflaged estuary that was known by only a few local fishermen. As he guided his vessel deep into the vast salt marsh, the fog intensified over the mazelike waterway, and Sharp's boat became invisible.

Sharp was determined to quickly return to the safety of his concealed boat slip behind his home. Even so, while he navigated through the narrow channel and high surrounding grasses, Sharp became agitated when his boat suddenly grounded on the shallow, muddy bottom.

Wasting no time to make his craft more buoyant, Sharp climbed out of his boat and stepped into the water. He then waded toward the stern and began pushing the boat forward.

Much to his relief, after a minute or two, the boat pulled away from the mud's viselike grip and began to float freely again. After pushing the craft into deeper water, Sharp reboarded and continued his journey.

By the time he reached the slightly larger waterway of the Leonard Thorofare, Sharp felt more confident that he'd escaped without detection. His worries faded further when he made one last turn and approached his secluded property. At that moment, Sharp realized that the onset of heavy fog had been a stroke of good fortune. The fog had blocked the moonlight during his getaway, making it virtually impossible for anyone to see his vessel.

Frank steered his vessel into his boat slip, which was partially hidden by a large tree and dense foliage. He disembarked and then silently walked up a slight slope toward his small house and barn. Once there, he was relieved that all was quiet on the causeway and that there were no passing cars.

While thankful to be back in his home, Sharp was upset

that his covert surveillance activities went so terribly wrong that evening. He never anticipated that a teenage girl would interrupt his mission, and he was perturbed that he did not find the so-called cave that the two boys had openly discussed.

In a fit of frustration, he muttered, "They're just boys playing stupid pirate games. There's no way they could have found it. It's just not possible."

As the hours passed by, Frank Sharp tried to ease his concerns about taking the girl from her home by rationalizing that his actions had actually been very clever. He reasoned with false confidence, "Pushing that girl overboard was brilliant. I correctly calculated that the chasing boat would stop to save her. It certainly did, and I was able to escape without detection. Yes, indeed!"

While getting ready for bed, he noticed a small scratch on his wrist. Thinking to himself, "Hmm, wonder how that happened," Frank went into his bathroom, washed the small wound, and then placed an adhesive bandage on it before heading for bed.

Given the evening's frustrating events, Sharp quickly fell into a deep sleep. Even so, a few hours later, Frank's body suddenly stirred, and he awoke in a confused state. As he sat up in his bed with his eyes wide open and a trancelike expression on his face, Frank hypnotically spoke the words "40 years … So close … Fatherland … My Führer."

Sitting alone in the dark, he slowly became conscious of his surroundings and then realized that he had just experienced a horrible nightmare. The subject matter was familiar, but on that particular evening, the haunted visions of his secret past were daunting and filled with dark and grave hallucinations.

Frank had experienced a ghostly visit from the Führer, who was enraged and furious at Frank Sharp for betraying the

Fatherland. "You are a weak man, Franz Schmidt! You've settled for the easy life on Seven Mile Island instead of serving Germany."

The terrifying apparition criticized Frank for his failure to recover the U-boat and for never reaching Argentina with the valuable cargo. With the Führer's eyes burning deep into Frank's soul, the eerie ghost made an incensed final pledge before disappearing into the foggy night. "Franz Schmidt, from now on, you will live a life of misery. You have failed your country, and you have cheated me from realizing ultimate victory and a new world order."

CHAPTER 19
LUAU PREPARATIONS

{Seven Mile Island – June 1985}

Later that morning, Dylan received another call from Max Thomas. "Hi, Dylan, I wanted to let you know that I'm finishing up the work on the bridge today. I'll definitely stop by tomorrow morning to inspect the bulkhead and to write a repair estimate."

While Dylan was a little disappointed by the delay, wanting the damages fixed as soon as possible, he responded, "No problem, Max. Thanks for the call. I know that everyone on Seven Mile Island appreciates your efforts to quickly repair the bridge. Be safe, and I'll see you tomorrow."

When the boys awoke, Grandma reminded them that there was another volleyball tournament on the beach at eleven o'clock. "If you two hurry up, you can grab something to eat and still make it in time to play."

As Wayne and Johnny rushed to change into their favorite nylon jogging shorts and tank tops, Liz called out, "Boys, remember to use suntan lotion. I don't want you getting burned in the hot sun!"

While darting out the front door, Johnny turned to Wayne and said, "Ya know, she was right about using the bug spray for boating. I guess we should grab the suntan lotion, too."

Wayne then yelled back, "OK, Mom. We love you. See you later."

Amazingly, during their rush to get to the volleyball tournament, the boys forgot all about their recent discovery!

When the boys got to the beach, they learned that they were not selected as partners for the day's tournament. Instead, they were assigned to play on different teams. While they weren't happy to be separated, they still believed that one of them could win a share of the grand prize gift certificate.

Unfortunately, this was not to be. At the conclusion of the tournament, Wayne's team placed second. Instead of winning a gift certificate, Wayne and his partner each received a flavored water ice treat. Johnny's team came in fourth place, which did not qualify for any awards.

Afterward, the boys were a little dejected about the outcome. Wayne sighed. "I wish we could have been on the same team again. We would have easily won."

Johnny more keenly rationalized, "Well, at least you won this huge water ice. Mmm, this is great!"

Fortunately, the boys were given two spoons, allowing them to share the thirst-quenching treat as they walked back to their grandparents' house.

After Lisa finally woke up, Christine and Elizabeth told her that they were planning to have a fun outdoor "Luau Feast" that evening. Secretly, the two women hoped that this would help to lift Lisa's spirits, given the previous night's traumatic experience.

"Honey, do us a favor and pick out some music to play at tonight's party," said Liz to her daughter.

After looking through her grandparents' record collection in the family room, Lisa selected the Elvis Presley soundtrack album *Blue Hawaii*. She had recently watched the movie on television and thought that the upbeat tropical songs would be perfect for the luau.

Lisa then went outside and walked over to her dad's Jeep. She climbed inside and grabbed his new cassette tape called *Jimmy Buffet's Greatest Hits*. After returning inside, Lisa described her music selections to her mom and grandmother. Liz said, "Those are perfect choices, Lisa. I know that everyone will enjoy the music."

A short time later, the ladies drove to Sharp's Fruits & Vegetables to pick up fresh produce and large shrimp. Frank was very charming as he spoke to the women about their luau dinner plans. Coincidentally, as they were paying for their selections, Liz noticed a bandage on Frank's right wrist. When Frank saw her looking, he quickly pulled his arm back. Then he politely smiled and said, "Thanks for your business, ladies. Have fun tonight."

As they walked back to the car, Grandma turned to Liz and said, "Frank is always such a gentleman. And his prices are very reasonable!"

On the drive home, the three women all sat silently. Liz pondered over the previous evening's unexpected event. She was truly frustrated that the police had not called with answers as to why her daughter was kidnapped. It simply made no sense. Liz was also annoyed with herself for having suspicious thoughts after she saw the small bandage on Frank Sharp's wrist. She thought, "He's just a nice old man. And he's my parents' friend! Come on, Liz, pull yourself together."

CHAPTER 20
GOLDEN BRICK

{Avalon, NJ – June 1985}

When the boys got home, they showered and then sat down with their dad and grandpa for a late lunch. After telling them about the day's competition results, Johnny turned to his brother and said, "Hey, Wayne, hurry up. We need to check out our treasure."

With one big gulp of his drink, Wayne gave an expression of great satisfaction and said, "Let's roll!"

In a flash, the two boys exited the back door and went straight to the dock's storage bench.

Wayne lifted the upper seat, and together, they pulled the gear bag out of the storage compartment and placed it down onto the wood deck surface. At the same time, Grandpa walked down to see what the boys were so excited about.

"Look what we found in our cave," said Wayne.

While Grandpa was somewhat confused as to what

exactly Wayne was talking about, he said, "Let me take a look."

Grandpa stared at the object, which measured approximately three inches high, five inches wide, and ten inches long. "I can't really tell what you've got there. Johnny, hand me the hose."

Johnny walked a few feet away and grabbed the dockside hose, which was generally used to clean the dock and boats. He turned on the water nozzle and handed the hose to his grandfather.

"Thanks, Johnny."

After adjusting the hose nozzle to produce a powerful jet stream of water, Grandpa aimed the surging blast directly at the dark, gooey, brick-like object. Together, they witnessed a thick layer of material fall off of the object.

"Wow, we found a crusty green brick," said Wayne in a somewhat sarcastic manner as he disappointingly looked at the object.

Grandpa then asked Johnny to go to the garage and retrieve a small bus tub and his toolbox, which were sitting just inside the door. Not missing a beat, he instructed Wayne to run up to the kitchen to retrieve a roll of aluminum foil and a box of baking soda.

Then he added, "Also, ask Grandma to boil some water in her teakettle."

"What do we need these things for?" asked Wayne.

Grandpa responded, "I have a suspicion that they'll help to clean this thing up. Then we can determine what you've really found."

After the whistle sounded, Grandma handed Wayne the teakettle and said, "Please be careful, Wayne! It's very hot." Wayne then walked slowly back to the dock with the requested items.

The boys watched their grandpa line the bus tub with a large sheet of tinfoil and then place the heavy brick into the middle of the tub. When he began sprinkling baking soda all over the object, Johnny asked, "Why are you doing that?"

"Baking soda's a mild alkali. When mixed with hot water and aluminum, the resulting mixture becomes a powerful stain remover. We'll know if it works in just a minute."

Grandpa asked Wayne to pour the teakettle's hot water onto the brick slowly. Immediately, it began to fizzle and bubble.

"Wow," said Johnny, "it's getting brighter!" Slowly, the tarnish and grime disappeared from the brick.

Grandpa continued cleaning the object with a small scrub brush, sweeping it back and forth to remove all of the crud embedded into its grooves and crevices. After pouring more hot water onto the object, the boys and their grandfather were very surprised to witness the rebirth of a shiny golden brick. Grandpa lifted the object from the tub and handed it to the boys, who dried it with a nearby beach towel.

Noticing some unusual markings on the object, Grandpa blurted out, "Whoa, slow down, boys. Turn the brick over. I want to see something." Gazing at the bar, he was astonished to see three engraved markings. The first was a picture of an eagle that seemed to be sitting on top of an unusual symbol. The second item was the word *Reichsbank*, and the third item was simply a series of letters and numbers.

Grandpa then looked very seriously at the boys and said, "Where exactly did you find this, boys?"

The boys offered an abbreviated explanation, stating that they had explored the crack in the bulkhead that was caused by the storm. Wayne added, "When we pushed the cracked board to the side, we discovered our Pirate Cave!"

Grandpa drifted off in deep thought for about thirty seconds before Johnny got his attention again. "Grandpa, what are all of these symbols on the brick?"

Grandpa looked soberly at the boys and said, "If I'm not

mistaken, you two have found a Nazi gold bar." Grandpa then said that the word *Reichsbank* was the name of the central bank of Germany up until the end of World War II. He went on to explain, "I think that these numbers are some kind of identification indicator."

Johnny then asked, "What's that strange emblem at the top?"

Grandpa responded solemnly, "Below the eagle is a symbol called a swastika. For hundreds of years, it was known as an ancient religious symbol throughout the world. Then Hitler and the Nazis rose to power in Germany during the 1930s." After taking a deep breath and shaking his head back and forth, Grandpa continued, "Hitler stole the symbol, just like a pirate!"

With a confused expression on his face, Wayne questioned, "What do you mean, Grandpa?"

"Well, Hitler's evil regime adopted the swastika symbol and used it for a different purpose. It was recognized by the Nazis as a symbol of German nationalistic pride. Hitler merged it with another historical German emblem, the eagle." Pointing to the gold bar, he directed the boys, "Look closely. You can see the eagle standing on top of the swastika symbol. That was the Nazi's national emblem from 1933 until the end of the war in 1945." Rubbing his brow in frustration, Grandpa added, "It was displayed on thousands of items, including Germany's money and currency. That's why I believe that you two have found a Nazi gold bar!"

Grandpa and the boys sat quietly on the deck for several minutes before Grandpa looked at the two boys and added, "I hope that you two understand that today, the swastika is considered a very ugly and evil symbol. It's a sad reminder of the horrific and murderous acts that the Nazis committed against millions of people throughout the world during

Hitler's decade-long reign of power." After silently holding the golden brick in his hands for about a minute, Grandpa said in earnest, "I'm sorry, boys, but Hitler and the Nazis make me sick." Then he instructed the boys to go inside because "the grown-ups need to talk."

While the adults were truly amazed that Wayne and Johnny had made such a huge discovery without their knowing, they also understood that this unexpected find could have great historical significance and potential political consequences. Dylan quashed any thoughts of keeping the gold bar when he said, "The boys found this gold bar on my property, but it does not rightfully belong to any of us."

After a lengthy discussion, the adults met with the boys and their sister in the family room. Mark placed the golden object onto the hardwood floor directly in front of the fireplace. For the next few minutes, the adults talked about the discovery of the gold bar and explained their concerns about possessing such an object. The adults advised that they had decided to report this incredible find to Grandpa's longtime friend, Mayor Carrington.

Mark added, "Kids, we absolutely have to disclose your discovery to the authorities. They'll be able to offer guidance as to the best way to handle this unique situation."

Soon afterward, the mayor and the police chief arrived at the Masters' home. They stayed for almost an hour and were absolutely amazed to learn the details about the find. Unfortunately, they weren't able to thoroughly inspect the breach in the bulkhead because of the high tide and the rapidly fading sunlight.

Before the mayor and police chief left, it was agreed that they would transport the gold bar to the police station, where it would be placed in the station's secure storage locker for the evening. Further, Mayor Carrington and Chief Grant agreed to return the next morning so that they could get a better look at what the boys called their Pirate Cave.

As the mayor and chief were walking to their vehicles, Dylan mentioned, "By the way, Max Thomas is scheduled to be here tomorrow morning to inspect the damaged seawall and to write up a repair estimate. He might be able to help us get a better look at what's inside the bulkhead cave."

The mayor responded, "That's good to hear, Dylan. Max is one of the best seawall contractors on the island, and we'll likely need his expertise and advice. See you in the morning."

As the family continued to discuss the astonishing discovery, Lisa looked at the clock and sighed. "It's almost nine o'clock. I guess that means that our luau is canceled."

In response, Grandpa said, "Baloney! I'm still up for a luau. And besides, I'm starving!"

Grandma then chimed in. "Lisa, let's hear that great music that you picked out."

With her grandparents' encouragement, Lisa walked over to the stereo system in the family room and started playing the festive music.

Fortunately, the fun tropical sounds that filled the air really helped to alleviate the stressful vibes that had overwhelmed the family for the past few hours. In fact, everyone seemed relieved that they were having the luau dinner.

Outside, Mark and Liz began grilling the large shrimp, fresh pineapple slices, yellow squash, tomatoes, zucchini, and green peppers. Meanwhile, Christine prepared a huge tropical fruit salad as the boys chipped in by pouring beverages for everyone.

In an effort to help lift Lisa's spirits, Grandpa asked his granddaughter to dance to a fun island song that had just begun to play. "Come on, Lisa. Let's see if you can keep up with me."

While Lisa was a bit embarrassed, dancing with Grandpa in the family room was the perfect recipe for bringing a smile to her face.

Glancing at his daughter and Dylan from the back deck, Mark whispered into Liz's ear, "Everything's gonna be fine, Liz." Then, looking down at the grill, he added, "Wow, this really smells awesome. I can't wait to feast on these shrimp kabobs!"

While the others were enjoying the moment, Johnny and his brother walked out to the dock.

"I feel kind of bad that our discovery upset Grandpa."

Wayne responded, "Me too. But I also feel bad that they won't let us keep the gold bar." After a short pause, Wayne added, "I wonder if they would have let us keep the gold if it had been a part of Blackbeard's treasure?"

Johnny dejectedly answered, "Probably not. Let's get something to eat. I'm starving."

Together, they returned to the house and joined the others, who had just begun eating.

CHAPTER 21
SHARP'S MISSION

{Seven Mile Island – June 1985}

The day after his clandestine mission to the Masters' property, Frank Sharp opened his market and attempted to perform his duties in a normal manner. As he worked that morning, his thoughts were torn between frustration and relief. On one hand, he was upset that the girl had unexpectedly appeared on the dock and that he had been forced to abduct her and then dump her in the bay. He was also disturbed by the frightening nightmare he experienced after his journey to the Masters' home. On the other hand, he was relieved that he hadn't been caught, and he rationalized that there was no possible way that anyone could suspect his involvement in the incident.

Regardless, it was business as usual for Frank throughout most of the morning. That was until he accidentally bumped his wrist against a table, which caused significant pain. It was also the moment when Frank remembered that the girl had scratched him when he pushed her off the boat.

To add insult to injury, at that instant, the girl entered his market with her mother and grandmother. While putting forth his absolute best demeanor to his customers and offering suggestions for their planned luau party, Frank could not help but notice how the girl's mother stared at his bandaged wrist as she paid for the fruit, vegetables, and shrimp.

After the ladies left the market, Frank decided that he needed to rest. He closed his business three hours earlier than normal and walked straight to his small house to try to get some sleep. Unfortunately, the more he thought about the botched mission, the more stressed and anxious he became. To make matters worse, he kept thinking about the girl's mother and the expression on her face as she seemed to look directly at his injured wrist. It was as if she was revealing, "I know that you're responsible for my daughter's kidnapping!"

After several hours of tossing and turning, Frank sat up in his bed and shouted, "There's no way she could know. I'm fine. I won't let that woman's silly expressions deter me."

Later that evening, Frank Sharp turned his focus back to the boys and their so-called Pirate Cave. He believed that the only reasonable place to search for the cave was at Dylan and Christine's large property. Because he had no way of knowing that the boys had already discovered a gold bar and that the authorities had been notified, Sharp irrationally decided that it would be safe to return to the Masters' home after nightfall to find the boys' cave.

Frank targeted 1:30 a.m. for his next mission, as he presumed that their luau party would be over by then and that the entire family would be asleep. After fine-tuning his surveillance plan, Frank reckoned that he had the perfect strategy to covertly inspect the property.

Noting that he still had several hours before he would embark, Frank decided to try to sleep. After setting his alarm clock, he closed his eyes and softly mumbled, "Please let me relax and rest."

As he slept, Frank's vivid imagination returned. He dreamed about his youthful past as a handsome, intelligent, and successful Kriegsmarine naval officer who was always willing to do anything for the Führer and Germany. The satisfying hallucinations reached a pinnacle when Frank envisioned that he found the U-boat with its valuable cargo on Dylan and Christine's property. At that moment, the sleeping man gave a sigh of pure bliss as he visualized himself navigating the U-boat toward Argentina.

The delightful dream was disrupted by the loud blasting of his alarm clock, which forced him to open his eyes and begrudgingly face reality. It was 12:15 a.m. when Frank sat up in his bed. After a brief moment to collect his thoughts, he felt refreshed and full of excitement.

Frank quickly dressed in all-black lightweight pants, a long-sleeved shirt with an attached hood, shoes, and gloves. After collecting his flashlight from the closet, Frank looked into his bedroom mirror. Approving of his own reflection and feeling ready, Sharp began to laugh in a disturbing and eerie manner as he uttered the words, "Tonight's the night we meet again."

Instead of taking his boat back to the Masters' property, Frank decided to drive his car. At 1:15 a.m., he drove onto the island and headed north on Ocean Drive. Upon reaching 12th Street, Frank parked on the side of the dark road. He then exited his vehicle and walked unobserved through the town's deserted public park situated between 8th and 12th Streets. After turning west onto 7th Street, Frank walked a short distance on the unlit road before he reached Christine and Dylan's property. Pausing for a moment, he looked down the long stone walkway and could see their house situated at the northwest corner of the island.

As Frank quietly walked toward the house, he confidently believed that he would soon learn the truth about the Pirate Cave and also the fate of his long-lost U-boat.

With his anticipation and obsession reaching a boiling point, Frank struggled to think clearly. Moving in the darkness, he silently whispered, "So close. It's mine."

At two o'clock, Frank began using his flashlight to search

for the cave. After finding nothing of importance on the southeast side of the large property, he headed toward the lagoon area. But unbeknownst to Frank Sharp, not everyone was asleep at the house!

CHAPTER 22
"I'D SURE LIKE TO SOLVE THIS MYSTERY"

{Seven Mile Island – June 1985}

As Grandma, Liz, and the children headed to bed after the luau party ended, Mark asked Dylan, "It's only midnight. Would you like to have some coffee on the deck with me?"

His father-in-law responded, "That sounds like a great idea. I'm really not tired, and we can enjoy this beautiful summer night."

As the two men sat at the outdoor table, Mark confided, "For some unknown reason, I have a strange feeling that last night's intruder might just try to come back for another visit tonight. While I can't exactly pinpoint why, I think it's best if we keep an eye on your property just in case."

Dylan responded, "I understand, Mark. I feel the same way, and I'd sure like to solve this mystery."

For the next two hours, Dylan and Mark quietly talked on the unlit deck while relaxing to the sounds of Mother Nature that carried over the bay from the vast wetlands.

At two in the morning, Mark heard a muffled noise that sounded as if someone was walking on the decorative landscaping stones that covered most of the bayside property. He tapped Dylan on the arm and pointed to a dark figure that was moving slowly in the shadows next to the dock. Mark then launched himself like a ferocious lion off the deck, directly at the intruder, as he yelled, "Hey, what are you doing?"

At that same moment, Dylan flipped the switch to the dock's powerful overhead floodlights, promptly illuminating the entire waterfront area. As he looked out toward the dock, he was alarmed when he saw the intruder swing a large flashlight directly at Mark's head. Fortunately, Mark avoided the blow by quickly ducking.

Mark responded by tackling the trespasser to the wooden deck. The momentum of the blow carried both Mark and the intruder off the deck and into the dark lagoon.

Dylan quickly ran to the water's edge and was relieved to see that Mark was using a full nelson neck hold to immobilize the trespasser.

After jumping down into the waist-deep water to assist Mark, Dylan yanked off the intruder's hood. He and Mark both gasped in surprise when they recognized the face of Dylan's friend Frank Sharp!

With everything happening so quickly, Frank Sharp had no chance to escape. He desperately tried to free himself, but Frank was simply unable to pull from Mark's iron grip. Before surrendering, Frank briefly looked across the well-lit lagoon and noticed the bright lights shining directly on the dark opening in the bulkhead. It was then that he surmised that it must be the entrance to the Pirate Cave that the boys mentioned. Out of frustration, he screamed out, "Es Gehort

Mir!" A simple German phrase that means, "It belongs to me!"

Promptly responding to an urgent phone call from Christine, Chief Grant and several patrolmen arrived a few minutes later. In short order, they read Frank Sharp his rights and then escorted him to the Avalon Police Station.

While in custody, Sharp exhibited behavior that was unfamiliar and strange to those who knew him. It was as if Frank were bewitched by his German past. For the next few hours, he spoke only in his native German. He repeatedly yelled, "Bleib weg von meinem Schiff" {Stay away from my vessel} and "Es ist fur das neue Vaterland!" {It's for the new Fatherland}. The arresting officers were very relieved when the disoriented and unruly suspect finally closed his eyes and fell asleep while confined to the station's holding cell.

At six a.m., Frank awoke and the police detectives took measurements, photos, and a tissue sample from Frank's injured wrist. While the police intended to have a forensic laboratory examine the evidence associated with Frank and Lisa, a request was never made because of the information learned over the next few hours.

Much to the relief of the Avalon Police, Frank Sharp was no longer confused and he resumed speaking English. In fact, he was very cordial when he surprisingly asked to see the police chief.

Frank must have realized the futility of his situation after Chief Grant explained that he was being charged with trespassing and that other charges were pending. Frank insisted on giving a formal statement right then and there. Surprisingly, even though the chief further explained to Sharp that he had a right to remain silent and that he also had the right to have an attorney present, Frank waived his rights to counsel when he declared, "I don't want an attorney. I just want to give my statement now!"

Over the next several hours, Sharp told his life story to the astonished police chief and detectives. Frank revealed that his true identity was Franz Schmidt and that he was a German citizen who had been illegally residing in the United States for many years. He confessed to killing Sam Sharp in June 1945, stealing his business, and assaulting and kidnapping Lisa Sanders. Everyone present during the interview was shocked by Sharp's amazing testimony and confession.

When asked by the chief, "Why did you go to Christine and Dylan Masters' property?" Franz admitted that he had recently overheard the two Sanders boys discussing a cave that they had found.

Although he had no way of knowing exactly what they were talking about, he suspected that the boys might have stumbled upon his long-lost U-boat!

"That's why I went to Dylan's house. I just wanted to see if the boys had somehow found my old vessel. For the past forty years, I've searched just about everywhere on this island to find it. But the one place I never searched was Dylan's large property."

After sitting motionless for almost a minute, seemingly deep in thought, Sharp continued, "I truly had no intention of hurting the girl. Honestly!"

The interview lasted a very long time because the chief decided it was important to fully understand how Franz Schmidt illegally established his new identity as Frank Sharp. Chief Grant also wanted to determine if the boys' recent discovery had a connection with Sharp being a German U-boat officer during the Second World War, whose ship ran aground near Seven Mile Island.

Even though Franz knew that he'd likely spend the remainder of his life behind bars, he still felt compelled to reveal the truth. Wiping the tears from his eyes, he said, "I am sorry. I was a young soldier just following orders and trying to survive. Now I'm an old and foolish man who is ashamed of my past and of my recent actions." After a pause, Franz then quietly added, "So many promises, secrets, plans, and lies... So little truth."

Chief Grant asked Frank if there was anything else he wanted to say before concluding the statement. Sharp quietly responded, "I'm so sorry." With his head hung low, Frank began crying. An officer then escorted the defeated man back to the holding cell.

While sitting in his cell, Sharp could not help but wonder what was really inside the so-called Pirate Cave. Knowing that the police chief had not offered any information about the missing vessel, the bewildered man said to himself, "Could it really be my U-boat?" While his mind raced, pondering everything that had happened, Sharp felt overcome with extreme fatigue. Within seconds, the old man fell asleep, knowing that he had come up short in his misguided personal mission.

Meanwhile, Chief Grant sat in his office and began writing his initial report. While deep in thought, he rationalized that it was best not to tell his prisoner that the two boys had recently discovered a Nazi gold bar within the breach of the bulkhead.

An hour later, the chief placed his pen and the incomplete report into his desk drawer. Rubbing his hands through his hair, the tired senior officer realized that he'd have to enter the cave in order to solve the mystery. Only then would he be able to determine if it was somehow related to the missing U-boat.

Chief Grant then left the police station and drove to Dylan and Christine's home.

CHAPTER 23
THE DILEMMA

At eleven a.m., Dylan and Mark met with Mayor Carrington, Chief Grant, and Max Thomas. After briefly discussing the unexpected incarceration of Frank Sharp, the men changed into their swimsuits and then climbed into the lagoon. They carefully entered the ruptured bulkhead and toured a portion of the underground chamber using powerful searchlights. After taking many photographs of the surprisingly large interior, they returned to the dock.

"This is absolutely amazing! Nothing like this has ever been found on Seven Mile Island," confided the mayor.

Max added, "Well, Dylan, I certainly have never seen anything like this on the island. Even so, be assured that the structure is firmly in place, and I see no evidence of a collapse or any pending property erosion."

The police chief then turned to Mark and Dylan. "Based upon our inspection this morning and the information disclosed by Frank Sharp, it's clear that while the boys did not discover a 'pirate cave,' they did find a sizable portion of a German U-boat!"

Dylan added, "It's unbelievable! Christine and I have lived here for forty years, and we had no idea that our property was sitting on a sunken U-boat!"

The mayor turned to the police chief. "This is truly an awesome find. We need to immediately rope off this entire property."

The chief responded, "I agree. I'll implement around-the-clock security until the appropriate experts can examine the vessel and its contents. I hope they can offer advice as to how we should handle this situation."

Dylan Masters expressed his concern to the mayor and chief. "Can my family continue to stay here?"

The mayor assured him that his family definitely should remain on the property.

Meanwhile, the two boys were quietly listening to the adults from their upstairs bedroom window. They were amazed that their discovery was actually a German U-boat. Wayne turned to his brother, and with a frustrated look, he said, "Ugh, considering that they won't let us keep the gold bar, there's no way they're gonna let us keep the U-boat!"

Shortly thereafter, the adults and Lisa gathered in the large family room. Noticing that the boys weren't there, Mark yelled upstairs to his sons. "Boys, come down here. We have something important to discuss."

Once the boys were situated, Mayor Carrington addressed everyone. "Well, it appears that you two boys have discovered something of historical importance. With this in mind, anything that we discuss today is absolutely confidential."

Over the next hour, the mayor outlined the incredible events that had taken place since Mark and Liz's family had arrived at the Masters' home nine days earlier. Everyone in the room was simply amazed that a U-boat was sitting under Dylan and Christine's property.

The mayor continued, "I also want you to know that I'm sincerely thankful that the boys weren't injured while they were exploring the damaged bulkhead and that Lisa wasn't seriously hurt by Mr. Sharp."

Lisa quickly assured everyone that she was fine and then expressed, "I just can't believe that Johnny and Wayne discovered a U-boat on Grandma and Grandpa's property." Turning toward her brothers, she added, "You two are going to be famous!"

At that point, the mayor interjected, "Well, not just yet. Any recognition concerning this find will have to wait. Remember, because of the historical significance and the pending criminal investigation, you are not to discuss this matter with anyone outside of this room until further notice."

Mr. Thomas then explained that the anticipated excavation of the chamber would likely take significant time and would require large equipment. "Because the project will require extensive digging under the waterline, we may need to install a cofferdam around the lagoon to ensure that Christine and Dylan's home is protected and the earth behind the bulkhead doesn't collapse into the bay."

Wayne asked, "Mr. Thomas, what exactly is a cofferdam?"

The contractor promptly responded, "It's really just a temporary watertight wall that will be placed around the entire lagoon. The enclosure will allow us to excavate the U-boat without worrying about the tidewaters covering the worksite during each high tide cycle. In essence, the cofferdam will ensure a dry work environment and will make it easier for the experts to review and analyze this important find."

Then, looking at the boys, Max continued, "Unfortunately for you two, this means that you won't be able to swim in the lagoon until the work is completed."

Chief Grant added, "Yes, and that also means that no one but the proper authorities will be permitted near the U-boat."

Wayne and Johnny acknowledged that they fully understood and would definitely comply with the order. Wayne added, "No problem, sir. I'm just glad that there's still a ton of fun things to do here on Seven Mile Island besides swimming in the lagoon!"

In response to Wayne's joyful declaration, the tension in the room momentarily lifted. Grandpa turned to Wayne and said, "You're right, Wayne; this island has many exciting activities that will certainly keep you and your brother busy!"

The mayor then turned more serious. "If anyone outside this room inquires about the extensive work, your response should be brief and somewhat accurate. Just say that Christine and Dylan's property has been roped off for safety reasons, and the bulkhead is being replaced."

With a serious expression on his face, Johnny coughed out loud, and everyone looked in his direction. He politely asked, "Mr. Mayor, is it really possible that the discovery of the U-boat on my grandparents' property could change history?"

The mayor responded, "That's a very good question, Johnny. What we know right now is that you and Wayne have discovered something that will definitely impact your entire family and our local community in the future. Depending upon the extent of the find, there is also the possibility that scholars, historians, and journalists may need to make a few alterations or additions to the previously documented history concerning World War II. We'll all need to be patient for the time being. But, if I had to make a prediction, I'd bet that your discovery very well could result in a few more chapters being added to the history books sometime in the future!"

Wayne pushed his brother's shoulder, and with a joyful expression, he commented, "Wow, that's awesome, Johnny!"

Chief Grant went on to explain, "Frank Sharp admitted that his true identity is Franz Schmidt. He was a Kriegsmarine lieutenant commander who served on an XXI-A class German U-boat during the Second World War. He claims that his vessel became disabled and grounded somewhere near Seven Mile Island during a great hurricane in 1945.

"Sharp said that during the storm, he somehow was separated from the vessel. When the storm subsided, he woke up deep in the marshlands located west of our island. Interestingly, he further claims that for the past forty years, he has continuously searched for the U-boat and its contents, but he was never successful."

Dylan commented, "Wow, I guess that's why he's always roaming the beach with his metal detector whenever he's not operating his store." Christina chimed in. "Forty years. That's long enough to make anyone act crazy!"

The chief quickly moved on. "Again, everyone here truly has to be careful not to talk about this find with anyone else. Please understand that Frank Sharp also said that his U-boat was one of four in a convoy that was traveling on a secret voyage to Argentina! What makes this so significant is that Frank claims that the convoy was led by Adolf Hitler!"

The police chief's words took the entire family by surprise.

Recognizing everyone's shocked expressions, the mayor added, "If everything that Sharp said is true, and the experts confirm that it truly is a Nazi U-boat, then you can bet that the impact on all of us will be memorable."

Chief Grant then continued, "When Sharp was asked about the whereabouts of the other three vessels, he said that he couldn't confirm exactly what happened to them." The chief cautiously explained, "Interestingly, Sharp did make it a point to say that he wouldn't be surprised if Hitler reached Argentina."

Shaking his head in disbelief, Dylan said, "Absolutely amazing! If true, this really could alter history."

The chief then quietly advised, "Another astonishing thing about his testimony is that Frank was adamant that all four vessels carried massive quantities of gold bars!"

At that point, Wayne nudged Johnny and whispered, "Wow! We may need more baking soda!"

Grandpa then leaned toward the boys, and in a low voice, he sternly said, "Settle down, boys."

Chief Grant finished by stating, "While Sharp's testimony was quite convincing, we've also scheduled him to take a polygraph lie detector test."

Noticing confused expressions by Johnny and Wayne, Chief Grant explained, "Law enforcement agencies across the country use polygraph testing as an effective tool to help determine whether a person is telling the truth."

Before leaving the house, the mayor advised that because of the unique and unimaginable find, he would be contacting his good friend, Representative Crockett. He explained that Crockett was one of New Jersey's representatives who served in the United States House of Representatives in Washington, DC. "I'll reach out to Crockett as soon as I get back to my office. With his help, we can ensure that the boys' discovery is reported to the proper state and federal agencies. Crockett has good relations with not only the US Navy and the Coast Guard but also the country's best maritime attorneys. I hope they can explain all of our options for handling this find."

CHAPTER 24
"THIS SURE DOESN'T HAPPEN ON TV"

{Avalon, NJ – June/July 1985}

Two days later, Representative Crockett and maritime attorney Don Harrison traveled to the Masters' home to discuss the unique discovery and pending situation. Crockett complimented the family for promptly notifying the authorities and pointed out, "Too often, people who discover items of value and importance care only about a quick profit. They try to privately sell their finds in hopes of making a big windfall. By doing so, they risk being exposed to adverse actions and dangerous situations. I'm very pleased that you chose a different path."

Attorney Harrison added, "The congressman is correct. There are numerous documented incidents in which folks tried to sell a discovered antiquity on the black market. Far too often, these illegal dealings don't end well. The sellers often face difficult situations with swindlers and criminals.

And if and when they're caught, all of the parties have been subjected to prosecution by the authorities."

Attorney Harrison then told the family that many rules could apply to lost and found property. "It's not always easy to determine who's the rightful and legal owner of a significant and historical find. Generally, in our country, there's a presumption that the finder of an item of value will get to keep it as long as the item is found on his or her property." He then added, "But this situation is different. Other parties could make strong arguments that the property rightfully belongs to them. For example, the US government and the state of New Jersey could each assert claims of rightful control of the wrecked U-boat and its contents since these items were discovered in territorial waters."

At that point, Johnny said, "Wow, I never looked at it that way. I just thought that the cave … I mean U-boat … was on Grandma and Grandpa's land. So, the U-boat and gold must belong to them."

Harrison responded, "Well, Johnny, based upon everything that we've learned, it appears that the U-boat and the gold have been sitting within the confines of your grandparents' property lines for the past forty years. Even so, when you and Wayne entered the storm-damaged bulkhead, you found the vessel and its contents immersed in seawater. Because of this, the government could argue that the U-boat was, in fact, discovered in territorial waters. And as such, it falls under the government's control."

Wayne responded, "You're right, Mr. Carson. The cave, I mean U-boat, was filled with plenty of tidal water when Johnny and I climbed inside to explore."

Harrison added, "Well, there are actually more factors to consider besides just the landowner and the government. Because the vessel originally belonged to Germany, it's possible that the East German or West German governments could request the return of the vessel. Any such claim could be bolstered if we find remains of German sailors within the damaged U-boat."

Congressman Crockett then remarked, "But since the gold was not actually a component of the wrecked military vessel, there are viable reasons for not voluntarily returning the gold to either German government, especially since the gold may have been illegally obtained by Hitler's regime."

In a very serious manner, Crockett looked around the room and then continued. "Remember, since the end of the war, we've learned that the Nazis illegally took unimaginable stockpiles of bullion from multiple sources. Often by using shocking, sinister, and inhumane methods. The sources included the banks of occupied countries, businesses throughout Europe, and individuals who lived in Germany or the territories occupied by the German military forces."

In a sigh of frustration, Dylan remarked, "This is indeed a difficult situation to fully comprehend. There seem to be personal, local, state, national, and international ramifications. Oh my, there may be no easy way to decide who is the rightful owner. I never in a million years would have guessed that the big storm back in 1945 would have washed a Nazi U-boat onto our property and then bury it under tons of sand for all these years!"

Crockett responded, "Unfortunately, you're correct, Dylan. This is not going to be easy. All of these potential scenarios make this complicated to navigate. And to add more salt to the wound, if this matter is litigated to determine the ownership and salvage rights, it could take years before it's resolved, and there's no doubt that the legal expenses will be astronomical to all parties involved."

At this stage of the lengthy conversation, Mark sensed

that his entire family was truly overwhelmed and exhausted. Accordingly, he stood up and suggested, "I think we all could use a break. Let's adjourn for now and meet again tomorrow. This will give us some time to think about the best option for moving forward."

As the visitors were leaving, Mark felt bad when he noticed Johnny's and Wayne's distraught expressions as they sat on the floor in the living room. His heart ached when he overheard Wayne whisper to Johnny, "I never thought that finding a treasure would make everyone feel so rotten. This sure doesn't happen on TV. All the cool treasure-hunt shows and movies end with the good guys keeping the treasure!"

CHAPTER 25
THE DECISION

{South Jersey Coast – July/August 1985}

After dinner that evening, the adults met on the back deck and tried to process all the facts. Having a better understanding of how the recent events had historical significance, Mark summarized, "So it's agreed. We'll continue to cooperate with the state and federal officials. While it might disappoint Johnny and Wayne, we'll also disclaim any and all rights to the vessel and whatever contents it holds."

Dylan added, "I agree. This makes the most sense. The U-boat and the gold bars represent a horrible time in the world's history … when that evil dictator's war machine brought fear, pain, death, and destruction to so many people through its invasive and torturous acts. I really want nothing more to do with it!"

Before they retired for the night, the adults explained their decision to the kids. Dylan further agreed to call

Congressman Crockett the next day to advise him of the family's preference to relinquish all rights to the find.

———

The next few weeks passed by like a blur. After the state and federal officials worked out a compromise for handling the discovery, the excavation efforts quickly moved forward.

Representative Crockett periodically phoned Dylan and Mark to provide updates. During one call, he advised that the East and West German governments were separately contacted and notified of the discovery. Within a short time, the US government received formal responses from each country. Surprisingly, they both forfeited any claims to the discovery and reiterated their full support of continued world peace and unity among nations.

Crockett commented, "As far as I know, the Germans simply want this entire affair to disappear. They don't need any more bad publicity about the war, and they are officially looking at this entire affair as one that simply involved a couple of amateur treasure hunters who stumbled upon an old, rusted war relic. Honestly, it's my opinion that they just don't want anyone believing that Adolf Hitler didn't die in his Berlin bunker in 1945. Furthermore, I find it quite intriguing that the German officials would not comment regarding the possibility that Hitler survived the war and took residence in South America."

As the days passed, various government experts carefully excavated the property. Then, late one evening, a specially modified US Coast Guard vessel secretly arrived at the Masters' property, where it anchored just outside of the cofferdam. The vessel's massive deck crane extended over the dry lagoon, directly above the uncovered U-boat and its contents.

In no time at all, these items were quietly transferred onto the deck of the vessel, which then cruised away from Seven Mile Island without any detection from the public.

The unique craft traveled in stealth mode about thirty miles south, where it dropped anchor at the US Coast Guard Training Center in Cape May, New Jersey. Once there, extensive efforts began to preserve and restore the historical cargo.

A week after the U-boat was taken away and the bulkhead repairs were completed, Representative Crockett called Dylan and proudly advised, "We have plans to temporarily display the U-boat at the base where it can be viewed by the public. It will remain there until the construction of a planned maritime museum in Cape May is completed. We want future generations to understand how Nazi Germany not only attacked its enemies in Europe and Africa but also threatened the shores of our nation. The exhibit will document how German U-boats sank dozens of merchant ships just off the coast of New Jersey during the war."

Further, he shared astonishing news. "I also wanted to let

you know that there was more than just one gold bar discovered inside of the wrecked U-boat. In fact, the experts located and recovered more than six hundred fifty bars of gold!

"The US Department of Treasury has transferred the vast treasure to the US Bullion Depository in Fort Knox, Kentucky. I've been informed that the high-quality gold bars each weigh about thirty pounds and are valued at 130,000 dollars per bar. That's over 84 million dollars!"

Dylan simply responded, "Wow, we had no idea."

Crockett continued, "Our government has pledged to deposit a generous percentage of the gold into an international fund designated to benefit the surviving victims of the Holocaust and Nazi oppression."

Before saying goodbye to the congressman, Dylan said, "Thanks so much for your phone call. We really do appreciate that you've kept us informed on how the government is handling the discovery. On behalf of my family, I sincerely hope that the government's pledge has a positive impact and that it truly helps the survivors."

CHAPTER 26
"I CAN'T WAIT UNTIL NEXT SUMMER"

{Avalon, NJ – August/September 1985}

After the work at the Masters' property was completed, the remainder of the summer was significantly less dramatic. The adults had quietly agreed to focus their efforts on maintaining a sense of balance and normalcy for the children's sake. Fortunately for everyone, normal life at the shore could be very relaxing and enjoyable, especially on Seven Mile Island.

Wayne and Johnny continued to have a great time during the month of August. The boys won two more volleyball tournaments and went swimming and crabbing almost every day. They were especially pleased when another local seafood market agreed to buy their buckets of crabs for the remainder of the season.

Mark expressed great pride in his sons when they gave him the remaining loan balance for the boat motor. "This is absolutely fantastic, boys. I'm really proud of you. Between your volleyball games and your crabbing sales, you two have become quite the entrepreneurs."

The boys wisely decided to save most of their summer earnings. Even so, they did plan to use a portion of the money to host a pizza party for their water polo team when practices resumed in September.

Lisa carried on working at the Fishin' Pier Grille each morning, and she thoroughly enjoyed spending her afternoons with her friends, either hanging out at the beach or riding bikes all around the island.

When Labor Day weekend finally arrived, the Sanders family began packing their bags and loading up the Jeep Grand Wagoneer in preparation for the journey back to Moorestown. But before they left, the entire family put on their swimsuits and trekked up to the beach for one last summer swim in the ocean.

It was a beautiful sunny day, and everyone had fun. The kids enjoyed riding waves on their floating rafts and playing bocce ball on the vast beach. The adults cherished their final summer walk along the shoreline, searching for their own treasures of unique seashells and colorful sea glass.

As the day progressed, the family enjoyed relaxing on their beach chairs while watching a regatta of sailboats racing offshore. The twin-hulled catamarans swiftly slipped through the gentle swells just beyond the surf line while racing around the expansive watercourse marked by three buoys.

The family also spent time reminiscing about the exciting events and activities that had happened since June.

Lisa mentioned, "Mayor Carrington stopped by the Fishin' Pier Grille for breakfast yesterday. He told me that Frank Sharp ... I mean, Franz Schmidt ... remains in custody at the Cape May County Corrections Center for murdering of Sam Sharp in 1945 and for kidnapping me! He also said that there's been talk that Mr. Schmidt might be deported back to Germany, but the mayor didn't have any other details."

In response, Liz looked at her daughter and said, "I'm sure that the authorities will do the right thing. But most of all, I'm just grateful that you're OK." Then, swiftly changing her tone, Liz added, "Anyways, based on everything you've told us, I think that you managed to have a pretty awesome summer at the shore. I love you, Lisa."

"I have some related news that you might find interesting," Christine added. "Yesterday, I spoke to the American Legion's post commander. He said that the ownership rights to Sharp's business and property were recently transferred to the Borough of Avalon by the court. Apparently, the authorities searched Sharp's Fruits & Vegetables after Franz was incarcerated and found the original owner's notarized Last Will and Testament. Interestingly, it specified that Sam Sharp's estate was to be gifted to the Borough of Avalon upon his death."

"When questioned, Franz Schmidt admitted that he hid the document after Sam died in 1945 so no one would doubt that he was the rightful heir."

Dylan remarked, "Wow, that's quite amazing since Sharp's property isn't even located on the island. Regardless, I wonder what the town will do with the property. Sharp's market has certainly provided great goods and services to the islanders for many years."

Christine continued, "I asked the commander the same question. He said that the town had already agreed to jointly lease the entire property at a very affordable rate to the American Legion Post and a local farmer. Together, they'll be working during the summer months to run the fruit and vegetables market. And because the Legion has so many members and friends who have agreed to volunteer their time and services, the new tenants have pledged to donate a percentage of all future sales profits to assist not only the island's storm victims but also veterans, military personnel, and other families who are in need."

With a huge smile on her face, Christine said, "Can you believe it? This is wonderful news for the local community."

Late in the afternoon, the family returned to Dylan and Christine's home. The mood had understandably become a little downbeat since Liz, Mark, and the kids would soon be leaving the island. While the kids showered and dressed in preparation for the long drive home, Mark and Liz finished loading their vehicle.

An hour later, everyone gathered in the living room, where they embraced and said goodbye. As Liz hugged her parents, she said, "I love you, Mom and Dad. Thank you so much for having us this summer."

Just as Dylan and Christine began expressing how great it was to have the family together for the summer, the telephone rang.

Mark picked up the receiver. "Hi, can I help you?" He stood in front of the family, simply nodding his head and repeating, "Yes," "Wow," "That's very generous," "Yes, sir, we definitely accept," "The boys will be very happy to hear that," "Thanks a million … uh, literally."

When Mark hung up the phone, Dylan asked, "Who was that?"

Mark said, "Representative Crockett wanted to let us know how much he appreciated the boys' efforts in finding the U-boat. He also thanked us again for promptly reporting the discovery to the authorities."

Elizabeth commented, "That's nice. Why didn't you wish him a Happy Labor Day?"

Mark answered, "Well, I really didn't have an opportunity. The congressman said that the government would like to recognize the boys' discovery at a ceremony that will take place sometime in the near future. They'll receive a large plaque and get their photo taken with the governor and other high-ranking military officers." Johnny excitedly responded, "That's awesome!"

Mark then took a deep breath before adding, "The congressmen also mentioned that because we acted with great honesty and integrity, and because we signed over all our rights concerning the discovery, the government plans to show its appreciation by giving our family ... that is, everyone in this room ... a small finder's fee.

"Mr. Crockett indicated that the fee is intended to cover the expenses for replacing the damaged bulkhead and for any inconveniences that we may have experienced during the excavation project."

Wayne looked curiously at his dad and asked, "What exactly do you mean by 'small finder's fee'?"

Mark responded, "Well, it's actually a very generous monetary gift from the government to our family." After taking a few seconds to calm his shaking voice, Mark continued, "We will be receiving a check for two and a half percent of the total assessed value of the entire discovery within the next week!"

Liz gave her husband a surprised glance and slowly said, "That's two million dollars!"

Mark said, "Actually, the check will be slightly more than that."

After taking a few minutes to fully comprehend the very large sum that they would soon receive, the family was stunned by this good fortune.

When the initial excitement and jubilation passed, the

family agreed that they'd make certain to use the money for good and meaningful causes.

Finally, Liz and Mark told their excited children that it was time for everyone to get into the Wagoneer and head back home. Although the children were thrilled about the cool news and they really didn't want to leave the shore house, they understood that school would be starting in a few days and that they had to go. So, after everyone exchanged heartfelt goodbyes, the Jeep drove away from the shore.

While en route, Liz asked the boys, "Did you two explorers really have a fun summer?"

Johnny responded that he'd had the best summer ever. Then, with a mischievous smile planted on his face, Wayne added, "Even though I had a great time, I can't wait until next summer to find an even more amazing treasure!"

The whole family laughed out loud before Lisa said, "Dad, please put on some good music!"

EPILOGUE

After the Jeep pulled away from the house, Dylan and Christine walked outside toward the lagoon and sat down on the bench that was situated near the water. While gazing westward and admiring the sunset across the bay, they noticed a large turtle silently swimming near the dock.

Looking at the water, Dylan quietly said, "Look at that beautiful turtle. It's so cool, calm, and collected."

Christine squeezed her husband's hand and responded, "You're so right, Dylan. Ever since we moved here, these wonderful and peaceful creatures have always had such a calming effect on me."

Dylan fondly reflected back to the summer of 1945, when, as newlyweds, he and Christine witnessed thousands of turtles roaming the island in the aftermath of the horrible storm.

After a long pause, Dylan hugged his wife and said, "They truly are cooler by the mile."

The End

ACKNOWLEDGMENTS

When I began researching and writing this book, my plan was to write a fun middle-grade mystery tale using Seven Mile Island as the primary plot setting. I also wanted to capture the excitement of the books that I read as a boy by Ian Fleming and Robert Arthur, Jr. They were masters of writing clever stories with realistic twists and turns that always kept my attention. Most important, the plots were never too far-fetched or outrageous. Their works inspired me to visit many places, try new activities, and write this book. While creating the story and artwork took longer than planned, I'm truly pleased to have completed this lifelong dream project.

I'm so grateful for the wonderful times I've spent on Seven Mile Island. From its welcoming sunrises to calming sunsets, this special paradise of sandy beaches, protective dunes, abundant wildlife, and clear coastal waters is beyond compare. It has brought great joy and inspiration to my entire family for almost forty years.

Special thanks to my parents, Dan and Pam Thompson, who not only shared their appreciation of art and books, but also for their unending encouragement and love. As longtime islanders, their fondness and respect for the island's delicate environment have been inspiring, especially their efforts to protect the nesting diamondback terrapin turtles.

I also want to acknowledge Michael Witt, John Grant, Charles Covington, John Langston, Judy Thompson, Kathy Krantz, Chris Hoare, the Montanari family, The Wetlands Institute, and Laura Reichert and Bonita Risley at the Avalon History Center for their remarkable, and greatly appreciated, assistance, generosity, guidance, inspiration and/or research efforts.

Many thanks to Amy Snyder for her editing expertise, constructive and insightful comments, feedback, questions, research, assistance, and support. Further, I'm sincerely grateful to the awesome team at The Paper House. The amazing efforts of Mike, Tiffany, Mo and Tara were instrumental in bringing this project to fruition.

I especially want to express my love and gratitude to my son, RT, for his youthful and honest feedback. His optimistic viewpoint helped me stay focused, and his commitment to our country truly inspired me to finish this book.

Finally, I wish to thank my wonderful wife, Kristin, for her love, friendship, patience, understanding, and unconditional enthusiasm, which helped bring this story to life. She truly means the world to me.

ABOUT THE AUTHOR

Dan Thompson is a first time author and illustrator who has captured the spirit of an exciting family adventure at one of the Garden State's celebrated barrier islands in his new book.

Dan was born and raised in New Jersey. After graduating from Ohio State University, Dan returned to Jersey where he married, had a son, and began a long and rewarding career in the insurance industry.

Over the years Dan has enjoyed swimming, boating, biking, hiking, and also writing and performing music.

Utilizing a lifetime of experiences, Dan is thrilled to introduce his new middle grade historical fiction novel, The Secret Of Seven Mile Island.